My Mother's Pain

25 years apart, still holding
onto their love for each other

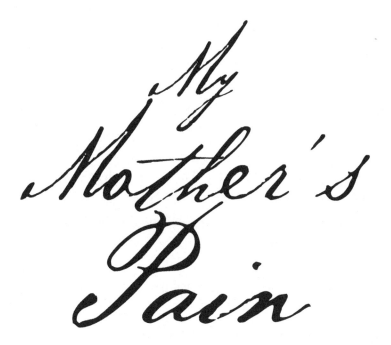

My Mother's Pain

**25 years apart, still holding
onto their love for each other**

A Novel By

FAE BIDGOLI

gatekeeper press™

Columbus, Ohio

My Mother's Pain: 25 years apart, still holding onto their love for each other

Published by Gatekeeper Press
2167 Stringtown Rd, Suite 109
Columbus, OH 43123-2989
www.GatekeeperPress.com

Library of Congress Control Number: 2020942492
ISBN (paperback): 9781662902673
eISBN: 9781662903007

Contents

In loving memory of Romina Ashrafi, from Northern Iran. Romina's father beheaded Romina in her sleep, in the name of Honor Killing on May 20, 2020.

Chapter 1

THE PHONE CALL...

She abruptly ended the phone conversation. Her thumb still pressing the red 'end call' button. Her hands were shaking. Her cell phone slipped onto the kitchen counter. Both hands caught her head as it dropped.

The room needed to be darker.

Her legs were trembling and didn't want to move. Finally, her pink slippers began mopping the floor, sliding along in uneven steps. She walked toward the open curtains in the living room.

Just before her daughter called, Jennifer had pulled open the curtains and noticed that the rain had stopped. She had smiled and said, "It's a good day to be out."

Her phone usually lay on the kitchen counter next to the coffee maker. She loved to check messages and return calls in the morning while waiting for coffee to brew.

Her pink slippers paused, and she stood in front of the floor-to-ceiling wall of glass, squinting in the bright sunlight.

What do I do now? she thought to herself.

She slowly closed the curtain, then moved through the now-dim room toward the couch. She shrugged off her pink robe and threw it on the loveseat across from the couch. Her pink nightgown, covered in small white flowers, danced around her naked body with each movement.

She hit her leg on the coffee table in front of the couch and winced, then reached down to gingerly rub the spot. Inching around the table, shuffle-stepping, she pivoted and dropped onto the edge of the couch. Her head sunk into her waiting hands as she leaned forward, staring at the Persian carpet. It seemed she was searching for the answer to her question in the small, colorful flowers of the carpet. She stared without blinking, and a memory surfaced of a time when her daughter Anita was about two years old.

Jennifer had taken her for a walk to the park that day and little Anita had made a discovery. The tiny white flowers that grew in the cracks of the sidewalk. She had plopped down next to them to get a closer look but wouldn't touch or pull the flowers.

On another day soon after, Jennifer, in a hurry, plucked one of the tiny white flowers and gave it to Anita, who grasped it with her tiny fingers, which seemed large compared to the flowers. It was obvious that she loved the flower much more than the lollipop she held in her other hand, so she gave the lollipop to her mother.

"Anita, you don't want your lollipop anymore?"

Anita shook her head. She was done with the lollipop. She then clutched the tiny flower with both hands.

From that day on, Anita often had a bouquet of the smallest flowers she could find growing in the cracks of the sidewalks. She would never touch cut flowers or flowers in front yards or at parks. Only the flowers that grew in the sidewalk cracks.

Maybe even at that age she knew that no matter how beautiful you were, if you grow in the wrong place, you could be stepped on and crushed. By gathering her tiny bouquets, she was saving the flowers from that fate.

Through her fingers, Jennifer mumbled, "No one can save me. I am crushed." And her tears fell silently on the carpeted bouquets at her feet.

"Where do I go now?"

Her body became heavy and she seemed to collapse, folding in on herself as her head bowed toward the floor. Her eyesight became blurry as all the flowers on the carpet dissolved into a dark gray spot.

Her lips were dry, and it felt as though something was caught in her throat. She coughed a few times, her hands dropping from her face to land beside her feet.

Suddenly, she sat up, straight and rigid, then jerked to standing and went to the kitchen.

Her steps were now quick and nimble, not at all like after the phone call.

"No, it can't be… It can't be…"

In the kitchen. Opening one cabinet after another, not bothering to close any. Searching. Soon all the cabinet doors were open.

Standing in the middle of the kitchen, looking at each cabinet, she turned right, then left. Then, she walked to the corner cabinet, left of the refrigerator. The cabinet held wine and champagne glasses.

Staring intently at the glasses, she picked one up and looked into it, her daughter's words rang in her ears but were interrupted by the memory of her excitement when shopping at the department store.

She took the escalator to the third floor, then walked through the aisles. A salesperson had come to her assistance.

"Are you looking for something special?"

"Yes, for my daughter's engagement party." She flashed a bright smile.

"Congratulations."

"Thank you."

Jennifer stood in front of a display of crystal glassware in a glass cabinet against the wall.

The salesperson asked, "Do you want me to unlock the cabinet?"

"Yes, please."

The salesperson, while opening the cabinet, took a deep breath and said, "Oh, I love weddings. It is a huge moment for the mother when her daughter gets married."

Jennifer put her hand on her heart and said, "I am very grateful. My daughter is marrying a wonderful boy."

"So, tell me what you are looking for."

"I am planning to have the engagement party at my home. We will be serving wine and champagne."

"An engagement party, how many guests are you anticipating?"

Jennifer closed her eyes for a second and replied, "Around eighty guests. I have some stemware already, but I would need another sixty wine and champagne glasses."

The salesperson took a wine glass from the cabinet, handed it to Jennifer and asked, "How about this one?"

Jennifer tapped on the wine glass with her finger, "It is not what I had in mind."

The salesperson took the glass back and handed her another one. "You will love this one; it's very pricy."

Jennifer took the wine glass, took a few steps back, and held the glass up to the light of the chandelier and said, "I love it."

The salesperson had a big smile on her face and said, "It will take me a couple of hours to pack sixty wine and sixty champagne glasses."

Jennifer added, "I also want a set of two of the best champagne and wine glasses you have in the store for my daughter and her fiancé. Please arrange for them to be delivered to my home."

Jennifer had been happy; full of joy and hope as she had unpacked all the glasses and stored them carefully in the cabinet.

Jennifer stood next to the cabinet, still looking at the champagne glass in her hand as her mind returned to the conversation with her daughter.

The phone rang, jarring her train of thought.

At first she ignored it, then suddenly she set the champagne glass back in the cupboard and hurried to pick up her phone.

"Jennifer speaking."

"This is Nancy – are you on your way? It's Monday. General meeting day with all the offices?"

"I won't be in today. Let everyone know. Please cancel all my appointments for today."

"Are you okay?"

"I am fine – just have a migraine."

"Do you need anything?" Nancy asked.

"No … thanks."

"Ok. I'll let everyone know you won't be in today."

"Great. See you tomorrow."

She hung up with her executive secretary, assured that her company would roll on as it had since she created it.

Returning to the corner cabinet, she picked up the champagne glass again, and in one fluid motion, smashed it into the granite counter. It shattered into tiny, glittering shards.

Reaching for the next one, she threw it – hard. It flew out the kitchen door and crashed onto the hardwood floor in the dining room. The third and fourth glasses landed on the kitchen counter.

One after another, she blindly threw the glasses, speaking words drowned out by the sounds of splintered glass. After the sixth glass, she was shouting. "It is not fair! it is not fair! it is not fair! I am in pain. I am in pain and I can't take it anymore!"

The brilliant stemware flew in every direction until only the pair of wine glasses bought for her daughter and future son-in-law remained intact. Glass shards glittered from nearly every surface in the kitchen, living room, and dining room. Floors, tables, furniture, the kitchen sink, and counters – all covered in jagged bits of glass.

She looked at the two very expensive crystal wine glasses. It seemed she was contemplating breaking these two. Instead, she grasped both in one hand, took two careful steps to the pantry, and retrieved a bottle of wine and a corkscrew. Then, she walked to the family room, tip-toeing to avoid the broken glass. Reaching the couch, she swept glass off the cushions with a throw pillow, then sat the bottle of wine and the matching pair of glasses on the coffee table, ignoring the glittering bits that lay here and there. Taking a deep breath, she extracted the cork, then sighed as the fragrance of the opened bottle of wine floated through the air.

She filled both glasses and immediately began drinking in long, measured swallows, one glass to the next, until both were empty.

Jennifer only drank alcohol on special occasions. Even then, she would only drink one glass of wine, and always with friends – never alone. She was alone now, and about to pour her third and fourth glass of wine.

She watched the wine flow, lush and dark red, into the glasses.

"My mother must have felt like this when she was crying. She must be feeling like this."

Gripping her third glass of wine, she drained it without pausing and set the empty glass on the table. She slumped and lay back on the couch, escaping into sleep.

The fourth glass of wine sat untouched.

ଔ ଔ

The phone was ringing. Jennifer opened her eyes, her gaze automatically going to the stylish clock on the wall. One p.m. She was late for her luncheon date with her friend, Jean. It was unlike Jennifer to be late. Obviously, Jean, waiting in the restaurant, had become worried and called.

Jennifer ignored the phone until the room was silent once again. Her headache had not abated, and her vision stayed fuzzy no matter how many times she blinked. After a few seconds of staring at the broken glass on the coffee table, the agony of her daughter's phone call gripped her mind like a raptor's claw.

The room began to slowly spin. She took several deep breaths, put a hand to her head, and leaned back into the couch cushions.

The phone began ringing again.

She couldn't stand the ringing. She staggered to the kitchen. It was Jean calling.

"Jean, I am so sorry. I completely forgot about lunch. I fell asleep."

"It's okay. What's going on? It's not like you to sleep in the afternoon."

"I had a few glasses of wine and I dosed off."

"Tell me what's wrong."

"Don't worry, everything is fine."

"I am coming over."

"No, please. I am fine. How about lunch at the same place tomorrow?"

"Are you sure?"

"Yes, see you tomorrow."

"See you then."

Jennifer shuffled back to the couch, dropping her cell phone on it before sitting.

She stared at the fourth glass of wine as though searching for an answer to some mystery. Her eyes slowly closed. Her arms folded around her midsection as she bent forward, her forehead finally resting on her knees.

"Where did I go wrong?" Her words, pitiful and breathlessly spoken, seemed to hang in the air. "Where did I go wrong?"

One arm slid from hiding to capture the glass of wine and bring it to her lips. She took a sip, made a face at the acrid taste and spat it back into the glass. Her fingers twitched, almost dropping the glass before setting it back on the table. Her arm dropped and hung by her side like a rag doll.

Staring again at everything and nothing, her mind spiraled through flashbacks of her childhood as jumbled words tumbled from her.

"…where did I go wrong…why didn't I see…I am done… done with life…this is not life…this is pain…pain…pain…I am done…done…"

Suddenly, her breathless murmuring stopped. A decision had solidified in the muck of her mind.

"No one will miss me."

A rag doll no more, she jerked upright, mind racing, full of speculations.

She thought of the different ways she could kill herself. She contemplated sleeping pills or a gun, but she couldn't decide.

"No, no. Killing myself is not the answer, but if that is not the answer, then what?"

Her eyes closed for two seconds.

"I pretend I am dead."

Two heartbeats pulse in her temples.

"I will cut contact with everyone I know."

In a split second, her mind began to spin, searching for ways to pretend to be dead. A brisk discussion ensued.

"Pretend dead… would I care what happened to my company? No. I would be dead. Okay, so they sell it. Pretend dead. Don't need this big home or all this fancy furniture. Do I keep it? No. I wouldn't know what happened to the home after me. If I have no company, no home, no interaction with family and friends – then what? Where would I go, being pretend dead? What would I do? I am only forty-five years old. How would the rest of my life be?"

A glimpse of escape lifted her spirit. She took three deep breaths, as though refueling, then continued brainstorming.

"Death is freedom." She nodded, then frowned. "But can I do that to Anita…?" She shook her head, then threw her arms about herself. "I must. So, I will pretend I'm dead."

Side-stepping the broken glass, she went to the window and pulled open the curtain. The whole city was awake, and she could see the Bay and Golden Gate bridges. She stared at those icons for a moment, then grabbed her robe from the loveseat, shook it a few times and put it on. Then, she sat down, facing the east wall where two enormous paintings hung centered on the wall, framed by floor-to-ceiling glass windows. Each painting was predominantly a vibrant red, like fire and summer sunsets and speeding fire engines all at once.

Elizabeth, her childhood friend and artist, whose paintings were sold in very upscale galleries, had given Jennifer the two paintings as a house-warming gift. She stared at the two crimson monoliths now, feeling that Elizabeth was her only true friend. She adored the paintings and the drama they brought to the room. The paintings were the focal point of the space, and the décor was based on them.

Elizabeth had predicted twenty-five years ago that Jennifer would end up unhappy. She remembered it like it was yesterday. *"Don't do it. You are making a big mistake. You won't be happy. Don't do it."*

"You were right, my dear Elizabeth. What a huge mistake. What do I do now?"

৪০ ৪০

In her robe, nightgown, and pink slippers, Jennifer took the elevator from the third floor to the garage. Going to the northwest corner, she pulled off a blanket covering a lateral file cabinet and opened the bottom drawer. It contained a pile of notebooks and letters. Under the notebooks was a framed picture of a young man in his early twenties.

She sat down next to the cabinet, reached for the picture, and looked into the young man's eyes. Her heart rate quickened, pounding rapidly. Time stilled. Then, pressing the picture to her heart, she whispered, "I still love you."

With that, she lay the picture in the bottom of the drawer again, then picked up the pair of red high-heeled shoes sitting atop the pile of notebooks.

After staring at them for a moment, she began to cry, and lightly touched the crimson toes of each shoe to her cheeks. Then she slipped them on, stood, and started to pace around the garage. There was plenty of room in the 4-car garage for her purposeful strides, as only two cars were parked in the space.

After a half hour, her sobs died down and she gathered up some of the notebooks and letters and returned to the third floor. She traded her robe for her raincoat, picked up her purse and cell phone, returned to the garage, got into one of the parked cars, and drove away.

Chapter 2

THE JOURNEY...

Jennifer parked in front of a small home. She wrapped her arms around the steering wheel and stared at the house. She was exhausted.

The street was quiet. The houses weren't particularly well kept. Paint was peeling, lawns overgrown. For sale signs sat in front of many houses.

The auction sign staked in the front yard of this house looked as big as the only window on the lower level. A couple in their mid-forties lived in the house. At this moment, they were standing behind the curtain covering the only window, peering at the car in front of their house through the space between the edge of the curtain and the wall.

"Rob, I think this lady is from the bank."

"I don't think so, Ingrid."

"Why is that?"

"Look at her car," he answered. "That car must have cost a fortune."

"Then why is she here?"

"She must be an investor looking at the house to see if it's worth her time."

"Should we go ask her what her plans will be after she buys the house? Maybe we can rent from her…"

"Honey, there will be so many bidders, she may not get the house. Investors want to buy for a fraction of the price. It's different than someone who buys the house because they want to live in it."

"I assume that's the way the rich get richer and the poor get poorer."

"I know, it is not fair. Let's go back to the kitchen and see where else we can send our resumes."

There was a sigh. "Okay, Rob. Let's keep looking…"

They turned from the window and went back to the kitchen. Rob returned to reading the employment section of the newspaper while Ingrid started to cook.

෨ ෨

Almost four hours had passed. It was beginning to get dark outside. Ingrid opened the front door to put the garbage out and saw that the car she had noticed earlier was still parked in front of the house. The driver seemed to be asleep, her head on the steering wheel.

Ingrid stepped back into the house and closed the door. "Rob, she's still there – something is wrong."

"Maybe she's lost…maybe she stole the car," he replied.

"Should we call the police?"

Rob looked at the floor for a moment, then said, "Let's go talk to her."

They walked out the door to the car, then stood next to the driver's side window and knocked on it.

Jennifer opened her eyes, saw the couple, rolled down the window and, without saying a word, stared at them.

Rob asked, "Ma'am, are you okay?"

"No, I am not," Jennifer said.

"Are you from the bank?"

"No, I am not."

"May I ask what you are doing here?"

"I don't know. I just drove here from San Francisco."

Ingrid jumped in, asking, "Do you know you are in Erie, Pennsylvania?"

"I guess so."

"Is this your car?" Rob asked.

"Yes, it is."

"Do you have proof?"

Jennifer turned to fumble with the glove compartment. The couple stepped back from the car door, not knowing what to expect. Jennifer pulled out her DMV registration, then took her driver's license from her purse and stuck an arm out the window, both items clutched in her hand. Rob took the driver's license and registration, then checked that all the information matched.

Ingrid leaned in to get a look, then said, "It's her car, and she lives in San Francisco."

Rob nodded, mumbling, "It's so strange." He handed the items back to Jennifer. "Do you want us to call for someone?"

"No, I don't want to talk to anyone."

Ingrid hesitated, then asked, "Do you want to come in for tea or coffee?"

"Yes, I would like that very much," Jennifer replied.

To Ingrid, Jennifer's response seemed sincere. Her thoughts were racing, trying to figure out what was wrong with this strange woman. At the same time, she also felt a pull toward Jennifer, almost as though she knew her.

She must be in shock; she must have lost a loved one.

As Jennifer attempted to get out of the car, Ingrid noticed that under her long raincoat she only wore a nightgown. She was also wearing a pair of red high-heeled shoes.

Ingrid took Jennifer's arm and they walked with Rob back to the house. It was a small home, maybe nine hundred square feet. Very small compared to Jennifer's five-thousand-plus square-foot home. The living room had one window facing the street, and there was a staircase leading to the upstairs bedrooms that faced the front door. Upon entering, a door across from the living room window led to the kitchen. The kitchen was just big enough for a table and four chairs.

As soon as Jennifer entered the house, she began crying. Rob and Ingrid were surprised at her uncontrollable tears.

Ingrid gave her a hug. "Do you care for a glass of water?"

"No, thank you."

"Then, what can I get you?"

"Nothing… I need sleep," Jennifer replied. "Can I sleep here tonight?"

"Yes, of course."

With her arm around Jennifer's shoulder, Ingrid directed the exhausted woman to their spare bedroom upstairs.

It was a small space with a single bed and a window facing the street. The curtains and bedspread were of a dark blue fabric with white roses, homemade, but perfect. It was obvious that Ingrid had put love and care into decorating the room. The sole personal touch was a wedding picture of Rob and Ingrid that hung on the wall.

As soon as Ingrid opened the door, Jennifer went to the bed and lay down before Ingrid could remove the bedspread, then pushed off her shoes and closed her eyes. Ingrid put a blanket over her, closed the door, and went downstairs.

Rob was waiting for her with a glass of lemonade. "This is for you."

"Thank you, I need it." Ingrid took several swallows of the cool drink.

"Is she asleep?" Rob asked.

"I think so. She must have lost someone. It seems she's grieving."

"We can ask her tomorrow. At least she isn't from the bank." Rob gave a grim smile.

"I almost forgot about our situation when I saw the pain in her eyes."

"I hope she gets a good night's sleep. A good night's sleep always helps to calm down the nerves."

Ingrid nodded. "What do you think her situation is?"

"I don't know. She drove in her nightgown and raincoat from San Francisco. Obviously, whatever happened, whatever brought her here, was sudden."

"Or maybe she is going to a funeral tomorrow?"

"You're right. Maybe her parents live here in Erie and she is here to visit them or go to a funeral," Rob agreed. "But then, why was she in front of our house for hours?"

"She's grieving… She must have lost her way to her parents' or relatives that live here – who knows?"

"Look at her car…she's rich. Why didn't she fly here instead of driving for several days?"

"That *is* strange. Guess we'll figure it out tomorrow." Ingrid took another sip of lemonade and sighed.

⬱ ⬱

The next morning, Rob and Ingrid were up early. They wandered around the house, as was their habit lately, looking at each other sadly.

"Rob, do you remember how much sweat you put into the remodel of this kitchen?" Ingrid said.

"Yes, my dear, I remember. This was our first home, and now, it seems it will be our last."

Ingrid took a deep breath. "Do you think we should ask Jennifer to help us? Her car is worth more than this home."

"No, Ingrid. That is not a good idea."

Ingrid pressed the thought. "I think the reason she has lost her way is the answer to our prayers. She is here to help us."

"This is a false hope. Be careful. We need to accept that we have lost our home."

The coffee was ready. Ingrid filled her best mug with the fresh brew and muttered under her breath, "Is it wrong of me to think she would help us? I need to be more concerned about her situation."

Taking the cup of coffee to the upstairs bedroom, she knocked on the door. There was no response. She hesitated.

It was eleven o'clock.

She'd slept fourteen hours.

Ingrid quietly opened the door.

At the creak of the door, Jennifer opened her eyes. For the first moment, she wasn't sure where she was. As soon as she saw Ingrid and the cup of coffee, she remembered. She sat up, then set aside the blanket Ingrid had put over her. Her eyes met Ingrid's. "Thank you for allowing me to stay here."

"You are welcome," Ingrid smiled and set the cup on the nightstand next to the bed.

"What time is it?" Jennifer asked.

"It is eleven a.m. Do you need to be somewhere?"

"No. Can I stay here for a couple of days?"

"Well...yes... but why here?" Ingrid asked.

"I don't know. I need to sort out my life."

Ingrid's fingers intertwined; hands clasped at her waist. "But why sort it out here?" she asked softly.

"I don't know, but if it is too much of an intrusion, I will leave shortly."

"It's no problem. You can stay," Ingrid assured her, then took a step toward the door and asked, "Do you need your suitcase from your car?"

"I don't have anything in the car."

"But you have nothing on except a nightgown and raincoat."

Jennifer looked at herself. "You're right. Why aren't I dressed?" She shrugged and added, "I need to buy some clothes."

"It seems you can fit in my clothes. Let me go get you something to wear."

Ingrid went to her bedroom, considering what might fit Jennifer, who looked to be a size six like Ingrid. Jennifer was a good two inches taller than Ingrid, who stood five-seven, and had black hair with brown eyes to Ingrid's blond hair and blue eyes.

Choosing the best t-shirt and jogging suit she had, Ingrid returned to the guest room and handed them to Jennifer.

"Thank you so much. I will return them as soon as I buy some clothes."

"No worries about that now. Let me show you the bathroom. A hot bath will help you feel better."

Jennifer entered the bathroom and closed the door behind her. She undressed and decided to take a quick shower, rather than a bath. Warm water enveloped her exhausted body from head to toe. Body beginning to relax, she suddenly jerked back a step, frightened, then quickly got out of the tub, the shower still running.

Her thoughts spiraled back to her childhood, to her mother's pain. And witnessing her tears over and over.

ৰু ৰু

Jennifer was five years old when she started praying for her mother to stop crying.

She remembered seeing blood in the bathtub and hearing her older sister Angela's scream.

"Mom, wake up!" Jennifer was sitting next to the bathtub, calling her mom, while Angela had run to the neighbor's house to get help.

"Mom, wake up… Mom, wake up…"

When she didn't get any response, she started to cry. Between her tears, she continued pleading, "Wake up, Mom." But there was no answer. She heard her two-month-old baby brother crying in the living room and ran to check on him. She held his tiny hand and said softly, "Justin, stop crying. Something's wrong with Mom. She's asleep in the bathtub."

Panic struck again and she ran back to the bathroom. "Mom, wake up! Justin is crying! Wake up, wake up."

Gasping and sobbing, she ran back to Justin, begging him to stop crying, just as Angela and two neighbors came into the house. One neighbor told Angela to take Jennifer and Justin to the upstairs bedroom.

Jennifer didn't know what was happening. She stood at the bedroom window and stared at the street below. It was winter and the street was covered with snow.

The night before, her mother had agreed, after Jennifer's continuous begging, to build a snowman.

"How many hours until we can go outside and build a snowman?"

"If you go to bed now, when you wake up in the morning we will go out and build the snowman."

"Before breakfast, early early morning?"

"No, we will go after breakfast. We need to eat a good meal to have the energy to build the snowman," her mother answered.

"Promise?"

"Promise."

She was looking at the snow and thinking about why her mom didn't help her build the snowman. "She promised, she promised."

"Who promised?" Angela said.

"Mom is asleep because she didn't want to build a snowman."

"She is—"

An ambulance sped up to the front of the house and parked, lights still flashing. Three men jumped out and hurried to the door.

Angela said, "Thank God they're here. I hope they save Mom."

"Angela, what happened to Mom?"

"You stay here, don't move. I am going downstairs to see what's happening."

Angela was on the last step to the living room and a neighbor saw her and said, "Let's go upstairs."

Jennifer was still looking out the window and saw the three strange men putting her mom into the ambulance.

"Mom, Mom, what's wrong? Where are they taking my mom?"

Jennifer's dad was always out working, except for Sunday. But that day he came home in the middle of the day.

"Dad, Dad, Mom was asleep, and those men took her. You need to go get her and bring her back. Dad, Dad, the water was red and Mom was asleep."

He took Jennifer in his arms and said, "Honey, I know all about it. Your mom is fine. They took her to the hospital to make her well. She will be coming back in a few days."

"Dad, can we go stay with her?"

"Not now, but we may go in a day or two to visit her."

"Dad, Dad, did you wake her up?"

"Yes, she is awake, don't worry. She is fine."

Five days later, her mom came home.

"Mom, are you feeling better?"

"Yes, Jennifer, I am fine. The doctor fixed me."

Angela ran to her mother's arms. It was such a relief that her mother was home and could take care of her little brother, Justin. After a big hug, Angela said, "Let me see your wrist."

"Why do you want to see my wrist?"

"I want to see the cut."

"Stop it," her mother said sternly. "Where is Justin?"

Justin was asleep. Her mom stood beside his baby bed staring down at him and whispered, "What was I thinking? What was I thinking?" Then she began to cry.

Jennifer tried to comfort her. "Mom, Mom, don't cry... don't cry."

"Okay, Jennifer. I'm not crying anymore."

80 80

Jennifer stared at herself in the bathroom mirror. A few times, she turned to look at the tub. Her nightgown was on the bathroom floor and she was fully dressed. Returning her gaze to her reflection, she mumbled, "What happened?"

She went back to the spare bedroom, picked up her raincoat and the cup of coffee, and walked down the stairs.

Rob was sitting in the living room watching TV when Jennifer came down. The screen showed Obama on his campaign trail. Seeing Jennifer, Rob stood up and waved toward the kitchen.

"Good morning, Jennifer. Coffee and toast are ready. Ingrid's in the kitchen."

Jennifer nodded and followed him into the kitchen. She sat next to the wall, facing the kitchen counter and sink. Quickly downing her coffee, she asked for another cup and Ingrid brought the coffee pot to the table to fill Jennifer's cup. Butter, peanut butter, jam, and toast were set on the table.

Rob was sitting facing the stove, sipping his coffee. He eyed Jennifer between sips, wanting to ask her about her life, trying to read her emotions to find the right moment to start his questioning. Ingrid sat opposite Jennifer.

A large picture of Obama hung on the wall. Jennifer had noticed it when she came into the kitchen. They all sat, attention on their cups of coffee, waiting a bit awkwardly for someone to start a conversation.

Jennifer took the lead. "I am so thankful to both of you for allowing me to stay here last night."

Ingrid said, "You're welcome."

Jennifer continued, "I see you are pro-Obama."

Rob quickly said, "I hope this man can change the way our lives have become. So much pain and so much unemployment; so much devastation."

"I also saw that your home is up for auction."

Rob nodded. "Yes, in a few days, we will be out of our first, and last, home."

"I am so sorry. How did that happen?"

Ingrid looked at Rob, who said, "Our home was paid off. I lost my job. The factory I worked at closed their doors. Since our home was free and clear, we managed with just Ingrid's paycheck. However, Ingrid was working for a very small company and they didn't have insurance. I became sick with cancer. We didn't have enough savings to pay off the medical bills; so, we refinanced our home. We were careful and made sure we would be able to pay the mortgage with Ingrid's paycheck."

At this point, tears filled both Ingrid and Rob's eyes.

Rob continued, "It's my fault. If I hadn't gotten sick, we wouldn't have had the mortgage and there wouldn't be a foreclosure."

Ingrid interjected, "Rob, what is this kind of talk? You getting sick is not your fault. We need to be thankful that we had the house and were able to refinance to pay for the operation and medical bills."

Jennifer, facing Rob, asked, "Are you okay now?"

"Yes, I am cancer free."

Ingrid took a deep breath. "Thank God for that."

Jennifer asked, "Then, what happened to make you behind on your mortgage?"

Rob gave her a grim smile and said, "We had spent almost all of our refinance money on the medical bills when Ingrid got laid off. As I mentioned, it was a small company...they couldn't survive in this terrible economy."

Looking into Jennifer's eyes, Ingrid softly said, "Enough about us. I want to know how you're doing."

Tears welled in Jennifer's eyes. She felt that it had been such a long time since anyone had asked about her feelings. She immediately got up and mumbled an apology, trying to hide her tears. As she left the kitchen, she said, "Give me a second and I'll be back."

She opened the front door to get some fresh spring air. She noticed the street was lined with plum and cherry trees; the pink and white blossoms providing a burst of color in the front yards of so many distressed homes.

Taking a deep breath to stop her tears, Jennifer noticed an approaching garbage truck, and was taken back to her third-grade school year.

ଞ ଞ

Jennifer would walk from home to school and back. She would wave and say hi to her father along the way as he gathered the garbage set out in the street for pick up. Angela was five years older than Jennifer and went to middle school, which was eight blocks further.

On this particular day, Angela's school didn't start until ten a.m. because of a teacher's conference. So, she decided to walk with Jennifer to her school, and then on to her own school. On the way, they saw their father. Jennifer's hand went up to wave as always, but Angela had grabbed it and said, "Come this way. We need to pretend we didn't see Dad."

"Why?"

"You don't understand."

"Why?" she asked again.

"Stop it."

Soon, they were at Jennifer's school. Angela said a quick goodbye and left.

Jennifer didn't understand why her sister had said to pretend they didn't see their dad until she was in the fourth grade.

Jennifer was playing in the school yard with a few of her class-mates. She clearly remembered the date, March 15th, 1973, and even the time – eleven a.m. – when her classmates started talking about their fathers.

"My dad is a doctor and works in the hospital," said one of her classmates. Another one said, "My dad is an insurance salesperson." Another jumped in, saying, "My dad is an attor-ney." Jennifer was about to say that her dad was a garbage man, when one of the girls said, "Jennifer's dad is our garbage man." Everyone started to giggle, and then they chanted, "Jennifer's dad is a garbage man."

Jennifer didn't say anything. She turned away and walked to the bathroom. She understood now why her sister, on their walk to school that day, pretended that they didn't see their dad. She went inside the bathroom and sat in a stall. She felt small, as if she was not one of them, her friends, that she was different.

While sitting in the stall, Jennifer remembered a night her father and mother were arguing. They thought the kids were asleep, but Jennifer was awake and had crept down the hallway next to the stairs. While shivering with fright, she listened to her dad and mom argue.

"Marguerite, if I didn't make the dinner the kids would go hungry. We have these kids now. We need to think of them."

"I destroyed your life, too."

"We need to forget about what our lives could have been if we had continued our education and I had a better job working fewer hours."

"I miss my parents and my sisters. I am angry at them and the culture that gave me so much pain, all because I followed my heart."

"Honey, come over here. Let me hold you."

"I know if they found out where we are living, we would be killed. I can't understand this culture. That a father could kill his daughter because she fell in love with a non-Muslim man, or for not obeying their wishes to marry an older man."

Marguerite was crying and Jennifer, still listening at the top of the stairs, couldn't take it anymore and ran to her mother. "Don't cry, Mom. Don't cry, Mom. You will fall asleep and have to go to the hospital again. Don't cry, Mom. Don't cry."

Jennifer promised herself that night, at that young age, never to quit school and to always be an honor student.

But at this moment, sitting in the bathroom stall, she couldn't bear to face her classmates. She loved her dad. It wasn't important to her that he was a garbage man. But the way her classmates giggled and made fun of her had hurt. And now, she felt different; like she wasn't one of them anymore.

She didn't want to go back to her classroom. She heard the bell signaling that class had started, but she didn't leave the stall. Her class was in session now. She had promised herself to be an honor student, and now she was missing class. The conflict made her miserable and she began to cry.

One of the teachers had come into the bathroom to wash her hands and heard Jennifer's crying. Walking to the stall, she softly knocked on the door.

"Are you okay?"

She didn't hear a response, only louder cries.

"It's Miss Robinson. Open the door."

Miss Robinson was Jennifer's third-grade teacher. She liked Jennifer very much, as she was such a good student and always behaved in a perfect manner.

When Jennifer heard Miss Robinson's voice, she opened the door, but continued to cry.

"It's you, Jennifer. What's wrong?"

Jennifer was still crying too much to answer. Miss Robinson directed her to wash her hands; then she took her by the hand and said, "Let's go to the office."

When they arrived at the office, Jennifer feared that since she had missed her class, she was no longer a good student. She thought she was going to be punished. She started to shiver and began sobbing anew. Then, the principal entered the room and Jennifer became even more frightened.

She was relieved when the principal said, "She is sick. Look at her, she's shivering. Call her parents to come collect her."

"Let's give her a cup of tea to warm her up," Miss Robinson said.

After drinking the tea, Jennifer stopped crying but was still too scared to talk in front of the principal. She remained silent until her mom came and took her home.

"What's wrong?" her mother asked.

Jennifer didn't know how to answer. She loved her father and didn't want to tell anyone about how her classmates had made fun of her because of her father's job. And now, because of her father's job, she had decided not to go to school anymore.

So, she didn't answer.

Her mother again asked, "What's wrong? Do you have any pain?"

She remained silent and put her hand on her stomach.

Her mother became impatient. "Is it your tummy?"

Jennifer nodded.

"Go to your room and stay in bed. You must have eaten too much junk."

It was such a relief for her to be in her room. That meant no more questions. She followed her mother's orders and stayed in bed. Her mind was busy with making plans on how not to go to school anymore. Being sick was a good way, but if she didn't go to school, what was she going to do when she was grown up? She would have to be a garbage woman. She couldn't find a way out and still felt bad that she was different from her classmates.

She missed her sister. She knew Angela would help her. So, she waited impatiently for Angela to come home. Angela and Jennifer shared a bedroom and a bunk bed that faced the bedroom door on the same wall as a small closet. The room was very small. No desk could fit in the room, so their books were on the floor next to the bunk bed. To the left of the bunk bed was a window to the street. To the right, on the wall, was a poster of Elvis Presley. Angela loved Elvis, and she would often tell Jennifer, "I want to sing like Elvis Presley. I will sing and the audience will clap for me and ask me to sing more."

When the two of them were in their room, instead of doing her homework, Angela would hold a stick like a microphone and sing into it. Jennifer would be her audience and, at the end of each song, would clap her hands loudly and say, "Sing it again. Sing it again!"

Jennifer stared at the poster and imagined her sister on stage singing, famous and rich, people clapping for her.

And Jennifer would be a garbage woman.

She heaved a big sigh and muttered, "No, I must go back to school. I am not going to be a garbage woman."

She got out of bed and went down to the living room. Her mother saw her and asked, "Are you feeling better?"

"Yes, I want to go back to school." She had her books in her hands and started walking toward the door.

"Wait a minute, you can't go now; school is ending in an hour. Come sit here and watch Justin. I need to wash clothes."

Jennifer obeyed and sat next to her little brother while her mother walked through the kitchen to the small sun porch, where Jennifer couldn't see her. Justin was asleep.

A moment later, Jennifer walked to the sun porch and stood behind the half-open door. She began watching her mom wash a huge pile of clothes by hand. She noticed how tired her mom looked, and in her mind, the decision to never have a life like her mother's was taking shape. She definitely needed to go back to school and never miss any class.

The next morning, on the way to school, she wondered how her classmates would behave when they saw her. She wanted to be in school but didn't want to face her classmates. Within these torn feelings, she remembered the time her sister told her to pretend that they didn't see their dad.

"Okay, I will pretend I do not see my classmates." She said this proclamation out loud.

It seemed she had found the answer to her dilemma and began to walk faster. When she entered school, her classmates surrounded her, asking what happened and why she hadn't returned to class the day before. But she was pretending she didn't see them. So, without answering their questions, she walked straight to her classroom.

80 80

Ingrid's voice interrupted Jennifer's thoughts as she stood in the open doorway. "Jennifer, are you okay?"

"Yes, yes. I am coming inside." Jennifer walked back into the kitchen and sat down. "I am so sorry. I am just so distracted."

There was silence. The couple didn't know how to respond. Ingrid finally broke the silence. "Jennifer, does your family know you left California to come here?"

"They don't know I'm here. I don't even know how I got here, but I know I left a message on my answering machine that I would be out of town."

Ingrid asked, "Could you tell us what happened?"

After a long silence, Jennifer said, "My daughter called early Monday morning, and everything lost its meaning in my life." Tears filled her eyes. She put her head down to hide her tears from Rob and Ingrid.

"I'm sorry I am so emotional." She reached for a tissue from the box on the table, wiped her tears, and stood up again. She was embarrassed. She never cried. The last time she cried in front of someone was in 1983, twenty-five years ago. That was the last time – and now she couldn't stop her tears, strangers or not. "I am sorry. Give me a moment," she said.

She took a few steps away from the breakfast table and faced the wall with Obama's picture, dabbing at her tears. She noticed a picture of a young girl in a Halloween costume. She stared at the picture, then took in a sharp breath as the picture changed and became one of Anita.

ಙ ಙ

In the third grade, Anita had decided to be a sunflower for Halloween. Since there wasn't a sunflower costume in the stores, Jennifer hired a designer and a tailor to make the costume. When the costume was finished and Jennifer saw the smile on Anita's face, she was beyond herself with excitement. It seemed she had succeeded in making her daughter happy.

At the same time, she remembered one Halloween when she was a child. She knew her parents didn't have the money to buy her a costume, but she wanted to go out on Halloween. She was dreaming of all the candies. Her sister, with the help of her friends, put on make-up and styled Angela's hair to look like Elvis Presley's.

But Jennifer didn't have a costume. She wore her sister's dress, which was too big on her. Her sister had said, "You are dressed up as a maid."

⁞ ⁞

Ingrid whispered to Rob, "Jennifer has been staring at Sandra's picture, should I interrupt her?"

Rob whispered back, "Best not to. I think her mind is somewhere else."

"I feel bad for her, but we still need to find somewhere to live. Our garage sale ad comes out tomorrow and we need to get ready."

"You're right," Rob sighed and nodded toward Jennifer. "Go tap on her shoulder and tell her we need to get on with our lives. It seems she has money, so she can go stay in a nice hotel in town. We can suggest that."

Ingrid got up and very gently tapped on Jennifer's shoulder. "Jennifer, are you okay?"

Jennifer didn't answer Ingrid, but instead asked, "Is this your daughter?"

"Yes."

"How old is she now?" Jennifer asked.

"Twenty-two."

"What is her name?"

"Sandra. She's in college. We are very proud of her. This fall she will be going back to school for her MBA. She is the first person in our family to get a college degree. Rob and I only have high school degrees."

Rob interrupted then, saying, "I just brewed a fresh pot of coffee. You two come over and have another cup."

Without answering, Jennifer and Ingrid returned to the table and sat down. Rob filled both their cups.

Jennifer took several sips, her brows furrowing, seeming to be deep in thought again. Then suddenly she asked, "You said your auction is in a few days, do you have the information about it?"

Ingrid nodded and picked up a small booklet. "Here's the booklet on it. They will be auctioning all of the homes in it."

Jennifer hadn't noticed the booklet before, though surely it had been sitting there since she arrived. She took the booklet and leafed through it.

Rob assumed she was looking for information about their home and said, "We're on page thirty-two."

Jennifer turned to the page and read the information.

Ingrid quietly said, "Pretty soon, we will be homeless. Our credit is so bad that our applications to rent a small place have been rejected many times."

Jennifer didn't respond. Instead, she turned to look at the booklet's back cover, then the inside of the back cover, and said, "We need a ten-percent cashier's check to be able to bid at the auction. We need to go to the bank and get a cashier's check."

Rob said, "Jennifer, we don't have any money in the bank."

Jennifer looked up from the booklet. "I'm sorry. I meant that *I* need to go to the bank."

Chapter 3

THE FABLE...

Ingrid and Rob's eyes went wide, and a glimpse of hope danced in their eyes. Rob swiped a tear from his cheek and asked, "Do you mean you want to help us?"

Jennifer gave him a blank look. "I don't know whether I am helping you two, or myself."

"What do you mean?" he asked.

"I don't know, but we're going to the auction. I'm buying your home back for you."

"This is huge," he said, still unsure about what she was saying. "But why would you do this?" Rob's voice quavered a bit.

"Just tell me, do you love your home?"

"Yes. This is our first home. We were high school sweethearts. After we got married, we worked very hard and saved our money. When Sandra was twelve, we moved here. Ever since then, every bit of money we had was used to improve our beloved home."

Ingrid quickly added, "Jennifer, we promise you, as soon as we start working again, we will pay you back. We will sign any document you need us to sign. We will pay you back, with interest."

Jennifer barely nodded, then said, "Now we need to go to the bank to get the cashier's check. After we get the house back, we'll talk about any arrangement between us."

Rob, blinking back tears, said, "Two days before you showed up, I had a dream and didn't know what to make of it. It was like I was in a valley surrounded by very steep hills. To get to my home, I had to climb the hills. But each time I climbed a hill, just before reaching the top, I would fall back into the valley. I would repeat my climb, but I would keep falling. Then I saw someone standing at the top of the hill. They had a robe in their hand. I couldn't see their face because they were too far away. Then they threw the robe at me and motioned to me to put it on. I do so and start to walk up the hill.

"This time it was so easy," he continued. "Like they were pulling me up. I had no fear of falling at all. Instead, I felt a calmness I had never before felt in my life. When I got to the top of the hill, the robe and the stranger were gone. It was like they didn't exist. And suddenly, I was in front of my home and all the lights were on inside. And then, I woke up."

Ingrid smiled. "Jennifer was that stranger, and the robe is her willingness to buy our home back, and the lights being on is the joy of homecoming."

Rob's brows furrowed. "What should we do about the garage sale?"

"We should cancel it," Ingrid answered. "If I have the chance to stay here, I don't have anything for sale. Everything I have, I need."

Rob got up and strode into the living room. His heart was pounding hard, his forehead and hands were covered in sweat, and he had trouble catching his breath. He recognized the symptoms of a panic attack and sat heavily in the chair near the stairs.

After managing a few deep breaths, he thought to himself, "I can't believe myself. I actually let myself believe Jennifer would buy back our home. She's not in her right mind. Her behavior is not normal. No one goes at the drop of a hat and offers to buy back a stranger's home for them. I need to warn Ingrid. She would be crushed if Jennifer doesn't mean it."

Rob hurried back to the kitchen, sat down, and, without hesitation, interrupted the conversation between Jennifer and Ingrid. "We need to continue with the garage sale tomorrow."

Ingrid's eyes went wide. "Why? When we get our home back, we will need our furnishings."

"You don't understand."

"What don't I understand?" she asked.

"Can I speak to you in private?"

"What is this about?"

Jennifer noticed that Rob looked stressed out and wanted to talk to Ingrid privately. Jennifer stood up and said, "I haven't seen the backyard. May I see it?" Before getting an answer, she opened the sliding glass door leading to the backyard and stepped out. Her first sight was the bountiful blossoms of apple and plum trees.

Her mind traveled back to the times when she and Angela played beneath the apple tree. When babysitting Justin, she would keep him engaged by playing with the apples that had fallen to the ground. Often, Angela would say, "Elvis is here to sing. Clap for Elvis." Jennifer would take Justin's tiny hands and clap them together while Angela sang and danced. A fallen branch from the apple tree served as her microphone.

Then Jennifer remembered her mother in the backyard, picking apples from the tree. Jennifer would often go to her parents' bedroom to sit on the bed and look into the backyard.

There had been a day when her father came home and, without changing out of his work clothes, he went into the backyard to find her mother.

She heard him say, "Marguerite, I have news about your parents. My parents met your parents."

Marguerite wore a frightened look and stopped what she was doing.

"Oh no, Christopher. How... When?"

"My parents saw your parents at a social gathering. My parents kept quiet and didn't talk to your parents."

"Where was this?"

"It was a cancer charity function. My parents recognized them from the pictures you showed them."

"What else? How did they look?" She bit her lip.

"My mom said they were fine, and from conversations with other friends, it seems they have pretended that you and your husband are living in Paris. They are claiming your husband has a very sensitive governmental job and can't leave Europe. And that every other year, they come to Paris to visit, since we cannot come to the United States."

"It is very clever. This way, they only have the shame of me running away."

Jennifer's father shook his head. "Maybe someday we can come back from 'Paris' and meet them again."

"I don't think so... Not as long as my father is alive."

Jennifer heard her father give a short laugh. "Do you think if I was a multi-millionaire your father would change his mind?"

"I don't think so. He is a very religious man and cannot accept his daughter marrying a non-Muslim man." She pivoted.

"Honey, I wish I had the millions. I would have shown you how I could change your dad's mind."

"I wish you did. I miss them so much, especially my mother and my sisters."

"At least with us being in Paris, your sisters can still get married."

"That makes me feel better. When did that charity gathering take place? And why didn't you tell me sooner?"

Her father extended a piece of paper to her mother. "Honey, here is the letter; I just got it from the mailbox. You can read it yourself."

While Jennifer was reminiscing in the backyard, Rob and Ingrid were deep in conversation in the kitchen. Rob's concern was evident when he said, "Ingrid, you know how much I love you... I'm afraid Jennifer raising your hopes will lead to disappointment. She is not in her right mind."

"Don't tell me that..." Tears flowed down Ingrid's cheeks. Rob took both her hands, his thumbs caressing her trembling fingers.

"Rob, I'm scared..."

"I am, too."

"What about the garage sale?" She flinched.

Rob put his hands behind his head. "Ingrid, we need to have the garage sale."

Disappointed, she said, "Okay, let's have the garage sale."

"We have a lot to do. Hopefully, the sale will produce a few month's rent at a cheap motel. And when we find jobs, we will be in a better position and someone will rent us an apartment."

Ingrid glanced at the door to the backyard. "What should we say to Jennifer?"

"I think we need to give her the addresses of a few hotels and ask her to leave."

Ingrid adjusted the lapels of her jacket. "But I told her she can stay here."

"Honey, she'll be okay. Now, let's call her in and let her know."

Ingrid hesitated, then looked into her husband's eyes. "I think you're right, Rob. She's not acting normal. It's like she's in a different world. She looks at me, but I know her mind is somewhere else."

Jennifer walked in and closed the sliding glass door behind her. "How far is Bank of America from here?"

Rob gave her the directions to the bank, as well as the names and addresses of three hotels on a slip of paper. Jennifer nodded, taking the paper. She understood that they were asking her to leave.

"Thank you. Ingrid, I will bring back your jogging suit as soon as I shop for some clothes."

Ingrid shook her head and said, "No worries. I would probably have sold it in the garage sale for pennies."

Ingrid followed Jennifer to the front door, where she hesitated for a second, then returned to the kitchen and asked Rob, "May I have the auction booklet?"

Rob immediately picked up the booklet and handed it to her. "Sure, take it. It's of no use to us."

Jennifer took the booklet, went back to the front door, and hugged Ingrid.

"Thank you again for your hospitality. I will not forget it."

Ingrid couldn't look Jennifer in the eyes. "If it wasn't for our situation, and the garage sale, and the auction—"

But Jennifer was already walking away.

She got into her car and drove away. She didn't drive to the bank, which was about three blocks from Rob and Ingrid's home. Instead, she went to the end of the street, a cul-de-sac with a community pool at the far end. Next to the pool was a path. Jennifer parked and got out of her car.

In moments, she was walking down the hidden pathway, which was connected to Lake Erie. Wildflowers grew along both sides of the path. Further out, to one side, was Lake Erie. On the other side was a tall cliff densely covered with trees and bushes.

As she walked, Jennifer heard her mother's voice. "Again, you came here by yourself. How many times have I told you? It is dangerous to be near the lake alone."

"Mom, it's pretty. Birds are singing."

"Promise me never to come back here alone. Do you understand?"

"Yes. I'm sorry."

Presently, Jennifer sat on a stone at the edge of the lake and stared at her reflection in the water. She didn't recognize herself. What she saw was an old, lonely, heartbroken woman with no emotional connection to anyone or anything.

She sat there for hours, staring at her reflection. Suddenly, she stood up and ran up the pathway like a deer bolting in fear. She had seen something that terrified her and needed to escape.

Reaching her car, she jumped in and drove away.

℃ ℃

It was about 6 p.m. when Jennifer knocked on the door of Rob and Ingrid's home.

They had spent the afternoon putting price tags on their furniture. The living room and kitchen were finished. All the utensils were tagged and laid out on the kitchen counter, along with their dishes and pots and pans.

They were in the bedroom now, with four suitcases ready to hold the things they wanted to take with them. Two sat by the closet door, already packed with their daughter's belongings. Ingrid sat on the floor next to the third suitcase as she read a letter Rob had written to her when they were seniors in high school.

'Ingrid, My Love,

Today I was walking near the lake. I saw the wild irises growing on the cliff next to the pathway. The deep blue color was breathtaking and drew everyone's eyes to that part of the cliff. I have walked there many times but never stood there in awe of the cliff.

It was the wild irises that were catching everyone's attention. While looking at the irises, I noticed so many delicate plants and trees that had been there that I never noticed. The different shades of green blending together in a harmonious pattern. The blue-colored irises gave life to that part of the cliff. And you are my blue iris. When I am with you, I experience life differently and everything around me smiles with joy. The joy and happiness I feel I never knew existed. I love you so much, my blue iris.'

Ingrid was about to pick up another letter from the same suitcase full of letters, cards, and gifts they had exchanged prior to their marriage, when she heard a knock on the door. She stood up and turned to Rob, who was lying on the bed, taking a break.

He heaved a big sigh. "I think people have seen the garage sale ad."

"Let's go let them know that the garage sale is tomorrow."

"Don't bother. They'll go away."

"Rob, during the last two years… why have you stopped calling me your blue iris?"

He opened up to her. "Ingrid, I have been so ashamed of myself. I promised to protect you, keep a roof over your head, and have food on the table. I have failed you. I don't deserve you or the honor of calling you my blue iris."

"Rob, don't talk like that. It breaks my heart."

Ingrid lay down next to Rob and put her head on his chest. Instinctively, Rob put his arm around her shoulder, his hand stroking her arm. Ingrid lifted her head and kissed Rob. Between each kiss, she whispered, "I can't lie; it's hard to give up this home and all of our belongings. But as long as I have you by my side, the joy of being with you quenches the pain of losing the house. Never talk like that again. *You* are my world, not the house. Do you understand?"

Rob returned her kisses with his passionate French kisses that had always melted her heart. She forgot about anything and everything else in her life.

After knocking at the door and getting no response, Jennifer went back to sit in her car and charge her cell phone. She started reading emails. So many of them were from her company's attorney and managers, and other work-related emails. She responded with a joint message to all:

> 'Hi everyone, I am out of town. In my absence, Mr. Jones, the company attorney, has the power to make any important decisions that need my approval. I must take care of a personal matter and am presently uncertain how much time my trip will require. I assure you all that I am well. The trip came up suddenly and I will fill in the details when I return. I will be unavailable for calls or emails during my absence. ~ Jennifer'

After she was finished with her emails, she went back to the door and knocked again, five or six times.

Ingrid walked to the other bedroom to look out the window that faced the street to see who was at the door. She couldn't see Jennifer, but she could see her car.

Ingrid called out to her husband, "Jennifer is at the door. What should we do?"

"Maybe the hotels had no vacancy."

"In this recession? No way. I feel bad for her; I told her she could stay here."

"If you want her to stay here, then let's go answer the door."

"She could help us tomorrow, during the garage sale."

They went downstairs and Rob stood next to the kitchen door. Ingrid opened the front door with a big smile. "Hi Jennifer, come in."

"I'm sorry, I couldn't go to a hotel. Please, allow me to spend the night here."

"Of course, come in."

Jennifer still wore the same jogging suit. It seemed she didn't go shopping.

"Jennifer, let's go upstairs." Ingrid led her to the bathroom, then grabbed another clean jogging suit and a t-shirt. "You need to take a bath or shower. Here are clean clothes, shampoo and conditioner, and no one has used this towel yet."

Jennifer, without answering, closed the bathroom door and undressed.

The hot water in the shower helped her shoulders relax and encouraged her to wash her hair. She decided to fill up the tub and soak in the warmth for a while.

There was so much on her mind. Deep, deep pain was surfacing and breaking the walls she had built around herself for so many years. The warm water was calming and eased the exhaustion in her body. She closed her eyes.

Moments passed, and then, in a flash, she envisioned her mother's arm on the edge of the tub and the blood dripping from her wrist into the tub, making the water red.

Panicked, Jennifer opened her eyes with a gasp, quickly rinsed herself off, and got out of the tub.

When Jennifer came downstairs, Rob and Ingrid were sitting in the living room watching the news about Obama. Jennifer was pro-Hillary Clinton and had even met her a few times at different fundraising events. The last time she had seen Hillary was in Los Angeles at a friend's home who was hosting a fundraising event. Considering the picture of Obama in Rob and Ingrid's kitchen, she kept quiet about this.

Rob said, "I hope Obama wins. He didn't grow up with a silver spoon in his mouth. He understands the needs of poor people. Look at us. My cancer and not having insurance caused us to become homeless. He is talking about universal healthcare for everyone."

Jennifer kept quiet and scanned the area around the TV, which was in a corner along the same wall as the entry door. There was a loveseat placed opposite to the stairs. Between the entry door and the TV was a chair, where Jennifer now sat. She had to turn her head to the right in order to see the TV.

The kitchen door was open, and she noticed all the pots and pans were out on the counter. Her gaze went from the kitchen to the stairs and saw that the file cabinet and the chair beneath the stairs had price tags on them. Then, she saw the price tag on the couch, loveseat, and the pictures on the wall. Even on the TV.

42

Suddenly, she felt extreme sadness in her heart. The air became heavy. She wasn't hearing the TV anymore. She wasn't seeing Rob or Ingrid anymore.

ಚಿ ಚಿ

It was Angela in the middle of the room, and she was pouring her heart out. She wanted to die and cried nonstop, screaming, "Elvis is dead! Elvis is dead!"

Jennifer cried with her, feeling her sister's pain. She tried to calm her down. "Angela, pretend he is not dead!"

"Leave me alone."

"Angela, please don't cry."

"He is dead. Elvis is *dead*. You don't understand, Elvis is dead."

"Angela, you can just pretend he is not dead. Then you won't cry."

ಚಿ ಚಿ

The whistle of the kettle in the kitchen jarred Jennifer back. She hadn't even seen Ingrid go to the kitchen to boil the water for tea.

Jennifer remembered how depressed Angela became after Elvis's death and how she never sang again. She started to miss Angela and wondered how she was doing now. It had been such a long time since they had seen each other.

Jennifer repeated very quietly, "She needs to sing. She needs to sing again."

Ingrid, sitting on the loveseat, turned to Jennifer. "Who needs to sing again?"

Jennifer looked up. "I am sorry, what did you say?"

"You said: she needs to sing again."

"It is a long story." But she didn't tell the story.

Rob, sitting on the couch opposite Jennifer, looked at Ingrid. There was silence until Ingrid said, "We have nothing to eat except peanut butter and jelly. May I make you two a peanut butter and jelly sandwich?"

Jennifer responded, "Let's eat out. Which is your favorite restaurant?"

"Jennifer, we can't eat out. We can't afford that kind of luxury," Rob said sharply.

"I am sorry. I wasn't clear. It's on me."

Ingrid, with very kind eyes, gazed at Jennifer. "Thank you, Jennifer. That is very kind of you; however, we are not finished tagging the bedroom furniture. We need to finish it tonight. I know tomorrow, early morning, our home will be packed with people."

"I thought you changed your mind about the garage sale?"

Ingrid answered, "No, we need to move forward. The sheriff will be here any day."

"I told you that I will buy back the house for you."

"Please don't say that when you know you won't do it."

"What do you mean? I told you... I will buy it back."

Rob snapped at her, "Jennifer, we know you are not in your right state of mind, so please don't play with our emotions when you know you won't buy the house back."

"I will," she stated firmly.

"Why do you want to buy a house here? Obviously you are rich, because you have a car like that," Rob said almost bitterly as he pointed toward the street. "You just met us. Rich people don't get rich by throwing away money."

"I don't understand. It seems I have made you upset."

"Of course I'm upset! Your car is worth more than our home, and now you're sitting here playing jokes on us."

Ingrid saw the tears in Jennifer's eyes and went to sit next to Rob, taking his hand and saying, "Rob, calm down. It isn't Jennifer's fault we're in this situation."

Jennifer stood up to leave. "Thank you for your hospitality. I will go to one of the hotels you suggested."

She picked up her purse and tried to find her car keys, but was too upset and distracted. She was about to empty out her purse on the chair when she saw the envelope. It was the cashier's check she had gotten for the auction. She lay it on the coffee table in front of the conflicted couple.

"I will buy the house back. Here is the cashier's check to allow me to bid."

Rob was overwhelmed and covered his eyes. Ingrid jumped up and hugged Jennifer.

Ingrid couldn't contain her excitement. "I don't know what brought you here. Whatever the reason, it has been by God's hands. My prayers have been answered. You are my angel; you are my angel."

Jennifer hugged her back and said, "I don't know why I am here or why I drove here from California."

"Thank God you didn't park in front of another house!" Ingrid said.

Jennifer's mood darkened. "Everything is so confusing. It is better if I go."

Ingrid took her hand and said, "I won't let you go to a hotel. Please, Jennifer, stay here."

Rob, his head down, said, "Jennifer, I am so sorry. You really meant it when you said you would buy back our home. I am sorry for not believing you. Please, forgive us and stay."

Jennifer took a deep breath and sat down, dropping her opened purse onto the floor. Everything spilled out, but she didn't bother to pick it up.

The room became quiet and Jennifer gave several furtive looks around, her shoulders hunched and her arms tight against her sides. She opened her mouth twice to speak, but it seemed her words were stuck in her throat.

Then, drawing a deep breath, she managed to whisper, "I grew up in this house. I lost my brother Justin here. He was five years old." She paused; her gaze flitted to the back door. "He was playing in the backyard and decided to climb the apple tree. It was summertime. A very hot day. It was painful, very painful."

Her head bowed, hands in her lap, tears freely flowing, leaving dark dots on the blue jogging suit. She made no attempt to wipe them away.

Rob and Ingrid listened silently.

Jennifer continued, "I pretended it didn't happen. My brother was dead. I pretended that he didn't…die…."

She was silent for a few minutes, then took several deep breaths and cleared her throat. Her voice was still soft, but no longer a whisper.

"I became sick the next day. I couldn't go to his funeral to say goodbye." Her shoulders dropped and she shook her head. "Or maybe I didn't want to say goodbye…

"For a while, every night before going to bed, I would pray that the next morning Justin would be calling me. Jefe. He always called me Jefe. Week after week, my prayers weren't answered. Then…" She stopped and folded her arms. "I told myself that Justin was traveling with my grandmother. Since they lived in California, I kept saying that one of these days he would be back."

She began to rock side-to-side and whispered, "But I can't pretend anymore. He died that day. He died… and his death brought so much grief to our family."

46

Ingrid went to her, kneeled down in front of her, and, her voice breaking, said, "I remember. My parents' home was a few blocks away. The whole neighborhood mourned the accident."

Hugging Jennifer tightly, Ingrid continued, "I can't believe it. It's you. The whole neighborhood is still talking about the multi-millionaire who changed her parents' and her sister's life. We bought our home directly from your parents. They talked about the home you bought them in Philadelphia with so much joy. Your mother was so excited and happy about moving to a new home... and that your dad wouldn't have to work."

Rob leaned forward and gently asked, "How did you become so rich?"

Jennifer hesitated; the question made her uncomfortable, almost sad.

Ingrid smiled tenderly at Jennifer. "I can't wait to tell Sandra that you're here. We told her about you. We wanted our daughter to understand that it's possible to have parents like us and become as successful as you are."

Jennifer didn't respond. She had stopped trembling and now simply sat and stared ahead.

Ingrid saw Jennifer's detachment and decided she probably hadn't heard anything she or Rob had said. Releasing her embrace, she stood and motioned to Rob to follow her out of the room.

When they got into the kitchen, Ingrid said, "Rob, forget about questioning her. She's not in the room again... She's not hearing us."

"Yeah, I agree." He glanced around the kitchen. "Right now, I'm hungry. How about we order a pizza for dinner? Maybe after she eats, she'll feel better."

"You may be right. I doubt she's had lunch... but we can't afford pizza."

Rob threw an arm around her shoulder. "We'll pay with a credit card. Hopefully it's not maxed out." He leaned in and kissed Ingrid's cheek. "I feel bad. It was insensitive to ask Jennifer about her wealth. She was in such pain and mourning her brother's death... maybe even for the first time."

"Rob, I know you and how kind-hearted you are. It'll be okay."

They returned to the front room and sat quietly for a few minutes, watching Jennifer. She was sitting with her head down now, lost in her thoughts. Justin's life, from birth to death, was flashing through her mind. She hadn't noticed Ingrid and Rob leaving the room or returning.

Finally, Rob broke the silence. "Jennifer, did you know that our home was foreclosed and being auctioned?"

Jennifer looked up at Rob and said, "No, I didn't."

"Why did you come back here, after so many years?"

"I don't know." Her eyes welled up.

Rob asked, "What happened to make you drive all the way here?"

Jennifer chewed her bottom lip. "A phone call."

"A phone call from whom?"

"My daughter..."

Rob was getting frustrated with her short answers. "What happened?"

"There was a phone call from my daughter... When I hung up the phone, something died in me."

"What do you mean?"

"After I hung up the phone, I felt I had lost my reason for living. I considered killing myself. Then, I decided to pretend that I was dead. The next thing I knew I was in the car driving. I ended up here."

Ingrid had always been interested in the way kids behaved toward each other. In high school, she was in the library almost every day, checking out books related to human behavior or psychology. She was most interested in how a negative thought or behavior could be changed to a positive one. She even took psychology courses at the community college to support this hobby interest.

When Jennifer said she had lost her reason for living after the phone call, Ingrid grew alarmed. She immediately jumped in and asked, "Jennifer, how do you feel now?"

"I am lost."

"Do you still feel like killing yourself?"

"In San Francisco. Not anymore." A flush crept up her face.

Ingrid pressed her. "What changed?"

Jennifer pressed her hands against her cheeks. "I am very good at pretending."

"What do you mean?" She shook her head.

"Pretending I'm dead. If I'm alive, I have to deal with my problems," she said.

"Like the phone call from your daughter?"

"Yes."

"What was it about?"

"I can't talk about it." Her shoulders slumped.

"Jennifer, I know a good therapist. I can call tomorrow to make an appointment for you. You need to see her. She will help you sort out your life."

"Give me the information. I'll make the appointment."

Rob spoke up at this point, saying, "Jennifer, we're glad you're here."

Ingrid leaned toward Jennifer. "It's the answer to our prayers that you're here." She caught Jennifer's gaze and added, "How do you feel now?"

"I won't be okay until I say goodbye to him."

"Goodbye to...?" Ingrid let the question hang in the air.

"To Babak…" Jennifer said, then shook her head, brows furrowed. "No, to Justin."

"Justin? Was that your brother? Who is Babak?"

Jennifer shook her head again, firmly. "No, I need to say goodbye to Justin." Then her voice grew softer. "I need to say goodbye to Babak." Her gaze was again at the floor, her head bowed.

Ingrid shifted in her seat. She wanted to break the mood with something positive.

"Jennifer, you have a lot to live for – at least financially. You are not like us not knowing each day if we will have food on our table. You don't have this kind of worry."

After a few moments, Jennifer looked up at them.

"I see you have love, the way you two look at each other. And you are there for each other. You have love."

"I am sure there are people in your life that love you, too," Ingrid said.

Jennifer spoke, but it seemed more to herself. "I have to say goodbye to Babak. I never said goodbye to him, or my brother."

"Tell us about Babak," Ingrid said, staring into Jennifer's eyes.

"I can't talk about him. It's too painful. I need to say goodbye to him." Then she abruptly stood up. "I'm going to bed. I'm tired."

"How about some dinner first? We ordered a pizza," Ingrid suggested.

"Thank you, but I am not hungry." Jennifer walked up the stairs with her head down. Her sadness filled the room. She was mourning the losses in her life and it all seemed to have started with her daughter's phone call.

Ingrid shook her head slowly. "She has lost someone named Babak…maybe he is her son?"

Rob rubbed his chin. "I don't think Babak is her son. Maybe her daughter called to say that Babak is dead. Maybe Babak was the father of her child or her husband or boyfriend. Maybe his death was such a shock it's taken her back to the death of her brother. And she drove across the country to say goodbye to her brother. Maybe Babak's relatives live here."

"Lots of maybes..." Ingrid said quietly. "But if relatives are here, why didn't she go to their house?"

They both sighed, then smiled and reached out for one another. Their hug reconfirmed the strength they had – they were stronger together. Rob nuzzled Ingrid's hair and whispered in her ear, "Tomorrow's a new day."

The last year and a half had been a trial. And now, they were placing their hopes on one damaged woman who came into their lives broken and wounded to the core. But that was okay. They were okay. And eventually, they would help Jennifer be okay.

Ingrid pressed her face into Rob's shoulder, muffling her words. "Let's put a sign on the door that the garage sale is cancelled."

Rob gave his wife a squeeze. "You read my mind. Let's get these tags off the furniture, too."

Rob took care of the cancellation sign while Ingrid put all the kitchen items away. When the last price tag had been pulled from the furniture, Rob grabbed Ingrid and kissed her, moving her slowly toward the kitchen pantry. Still in his arms, Ingrid opened the pantry door and took out a bottle of red wine. It was the only thing in the entire cabinet, saved for the first night after they were kicked out of their home, in hopes it might subdue the pain that they had no job, no home, and just enough money for a few months in a cheap motel.

Rob took the bottle from Ingrid and whispered in her ear, "Let's drink it tonight."

🙖 🙖

The next morning, after waking, Ingrid knocked on Jennifer's door. There was no answer. Opening the door, she saw that the bed was made, but no sign of Jennifer. She checked the bathroom – nothing. She hurried downstairs, glancing into the living room as she ran into the kitchen, and then out into the yard.

Gasping, she ran back inside and flung open the front door. Jennifer's car was gone.

Ingrid screamed at the top of her lungs, "Rob! Rob! Jennifer is gone!"

Rob hurried to her side and looked out to the street. "She'll be back."

"I have a bad feeling. Her bed was made."

He gave her a tired, but soft smile. "Let's not jump to conclusions."

"Do you think she is still going to the auction?"

Rob nodded. "Let's hope."

With his arm comfortingly around her shoulders, Rob guided her to the kitchen. She started a pot of coffee. Rob opened the refrigerator and plucked the last 3 eggs from the door keeper. When he closed the door, he noticed a note posted on the refrigerator. It was almost hidden among all the pictures of Sandra and Mother's and Father's Day cards from her.

The note was from Jennifer. Rob said, "Ingrid, come see – here is a note from Jennifer. I told you she would be back."

"What does it say?"

Rob read the note aloud: *I am on my way to saying goodbye. As I promised, I will show up at the auction. Thank you for allowing me to stay here. ~ Jennifer*

"Rob, she is not coming back. We asked her too many questions."

52

"Ingrid…don't worry. We don't know what her plans are. She may need to be with Babak's family."

Ingrid nodded.

"Sit down, my blue iris. I am making you an omelet."

ಬ ಬ

It had been early morning when Jennifer walked out of the house. While closing the door, she noticed the garage sale cancelation sign. She looked at the sign and smiled, then took a deep breath and walked to her car.

She didn't have any destination; she just drove around Ingrid and Rob's neighborhood. She saw Rob and Ingrid's garage sale signs still on streetlight poles and decided she would stop and would take each one down.

As she explored the area, she noticed a farmer's market and stopped in. She walked up and down the market aisles, feeling the need to be around people. It wasn't a large market like the one she was familiar with in San Francisco, near the ferry building. It took up just one small block and it was all produce, no crafts or any other merchandise. It was busy and crowded; no one paid attention to her.

She had walked through the market without buying anything for half an hour. Then she remembered Ingrid and Rob's refrigerator and all the empty shelves she had seen when Ingrid had taken milk out for coffee. She smiled, turned to the first vendor, and bought what they were offering. From there, she continued to the second and third vendors and bought vegetables, eggs, honey, nuts, fruit, and bread. She continued shopping and made a few trips to her car to load the groceries, until the trunk was packed with produce.

She drove through the town with no destination in mind again and ended up in front of a flea market. She parked her car on the street.

While walking down the steps that led to the flea market, Jennifer remembered Angela crying in front of an Elvis poster at the same flea market years ago, begging their mother, "Mom, Mom, *please* buy me this poster. It's Elvis!"

"What do you want to do with it?" asked their mother.

"I want to hang it in my room. Please! Please!"

"Not this time."

"But I can sing *just* like Elvis."

"I am sure you can, but not now."

"Please, Mom. I can sing for you now."

"No, Angela, another time."

"They'll sell it to someone else if we don't buy it."

"I'm sorry, Angela. I don't have enough money to buy the poster today."

Jennifer remembered how frightened she was while holding Angela's hand, enough to say, "Angela, it's just a poster. Don't make Mommy upset. She will cry. Don't make her upset."

"Stop it. You don't understand."

It was the last week that the kids were out of school. They were at the flea market to buy school clothes. Jennifer would be starting preschool.

A little while later, a solution to Angela's distress suddenly came to Jennifer. She took her mom's hand and said, "Mom, I don't need new clothes. I don't want any. Buy Angela that man's picture instead."

While they were standing in front of the shop and their mom was looking at pants for Jennifer, someone else bought the poster. Jennifer felt the excruciating pain her sister felt when the poster was rolled up and given to a young boy who wore a big smile on his face as he walked away with it. She also saw the tears in her mother's eyes when she took Angela in her arms and said, "I wish I could buy it for you. I promise I will buy an Elvis poster for you pretty soon."

Angela also saw her mother's tears, and suddenly the poster wasn't important anymore. She hugged her mom. "I'm sorry."

When Christmas came that year, Angela opened up her big present, the same Elvis poster. Angela was beyond herself with joy and Jennifer thought about how much her mom loved them and how smart she was to find that boy at the flea market and buy the poster back from him.

The produce in the car came to mind and Jennifer, without going into the flea market, went back to her car and drove away.

She delivered the produce to Ingrid and Rob and was about to leave when Ingrid asked, "Have you eaten anything?"

"Yes, I had a latte and a croissant," she answered.

"That is not breakfast. Come in; let me fix you something to eat."

"Thank you, but I am not hungry. I need to go…to say goodbye."

"Please come back tonight. With all this wonderful produce I will make something for dinner."

"I will. See you tonight."

Jennifer got into her car and drove away. Again, she was driving around the city from one street to another. She knew that she wanted to go to the cemetery, but though she knew where the cemetery was and drove down that street many times, she didn't stop the car.

Her mind was busy with memories.

Chapter 4

THE BEGINNING...

She hadn't felt joy for so many years, but today, when she delivered the produce to Ingrid and Rob, their excitement and the joy she saw in their eyes brought a ray of sunshine into her heart. She had felt the same joy when she saw the cancellation sign on the front of their house.

Her mind took her back to when she was accepted into UC Berkeley as an art major and how joyous she had felt. She remembered when she was in college her dream was to be an art teacher. She and her best friend and roommate, Elizabeth, were working on an art project. They would laugh for hours. Both wanted to finish college, get their teaching credentials, and become high school art teachers. Jennifer's goal was to come back and teach in Erie's public school. She believed in the idea that art connects us to our souls and that connection brings us joy and happiness.

Jennifer had always loved to paint, and every chance she had she would draw or paint, whether it was a portrait of Angela or her parents or the trees and flowers in their garden.

She continued to drive around, not bringing herself to stop at the cemetery.

She stopped at the art store and bought canvases and art supplies. While handing her credit card to the cashier, she smiled again. She put one of the canvases with a few brushes and the paint tubs in the front seat of her car. The rest of the canvasses were stowed in the trunk.

She drove on; finally stopping at the cemetery. She walked through the iron gate. The cemetery had changed so much it was almost unrecognizable. It was also crowded with people. There was a huge gathering that caught her eye for a moment.

She remembered Justin's grave was to the right of the iron gate, on the same side as the viewing room. And it was in the fifth row. Each row had a cherry tree at the beginning of the row. She walked along the cherry trees – one, two, three, four, five. She remembered the cherry trees and how small they were then. Now they were huge and in full bloom, each creating a broad canopy of shade. She turned right at the fifth row, reading each gravestone. She went up and down the row twice but couldn't find Justin.

She sat on the grass between the graves and started to cry. "It can't be, it can't be…" she said softly. "Which one of these graves is my brother's? Why didn't I come sooner?" Her grief deepened with each moment. Guilt added to her pain.

After a while, she decided to get her canvas and paint supplies. While walking back, she noticed, in the first row behind the viewing room, a huge tree stump. "This must be the first tree!"

With joy, she ran to the fourth cherry tree and turned right. In the middle of the row, on the right-hand side, she found her brother's grave.

Grass had grown up around it. No one had been there for a long time. The flower holder next to the grave was full of dirt, and the gravestone was muddy. It seemed even the rain couldn't wash the dirt from the stone. Sitting next to the grave, she took tissues from her pocket and cleaned the stone, then emptied out the flower box. Then she quickly got up, hurried to her car, and left the cemetery.

An hour later, she came back with fresh flowers and the proper tools to cut the grass around the grave. With paper towels, a brush, and the bottle of water she had, she washed the stone. She poured the rest of the water into the flower holder and put some of the cut flowers in there, placing potted orchids around the grave. As the last touch, she placed the rest of the cut flowers on top of the grave.

She sat there for a while, then went to her car and brought back the canvas and brushes. She didn't see or hear the other activities in the cemetery. She didn't even hear the cries of a young mother sitting in the row behind her.

A memory came to her. She had never eaten an apple. She had never touched one or ever bought apples. Even her friends had noticed, and in their gatherings never served apples in the fruit bowl or served apple pie. Her friends didn't know why Jennifer would stare at the apples in the fruit bowl and tune out until someone called her name. She would always say, "I'm sorry. My mind went somewhere else." It took a while to figure out that Jennifer's brother had died after falling from an apple tree.

It was a sunny day and the spring weather brought a very pleasant, gentle breeze. The brush was moving on the canvas along with Jennifer's emotions about losing Justin. She was not thinking about what she wanted to paint. This was the first time in twenty-five years she had a brush in her hand and a canvas before her. At times, a teardrop would hit the canvas and become part of her painting.

Hours had passed until it was early afternoon. She was the only one sitting on the damp grass between the rows of graves. From a distance, the tubes of paint on the grass looked like colorful flowers that had grown between the graves. Jennifer's mind went back to her early painting.

"I wish I hadn't told my mom to throw out my paintings when they moved to Philadelphia. What was I thinking? Justin's portrait was among those paintings." After Justin's death, she had hidden his portrait, not wanting her mother to see it and cry.

Jennifer never went to the backyard to play after Justin's death, and even when she had to be there, she always closed her eyes when facing the apple tree.

Jennifer was in a trance. She wasn't seeing her brush on the canvas or the colors she chose. Her red shoes were off her feet, laying on the grass. The blisters on her toes were obvious but she didn't feel them.

At about four p.m., she started to get hungry.

Without looking at the painting, she picked up the canvas, her brushes and paint tubes, and her shoes and walked barefoot to her car. She put her red shoes on the front seat and the canvas and the rest of her stuff in the backseat.

Ingrid and Rob heard the doorbell and went from the kitchen to the front door, all smiles. Since morning, they had worked nonstop. They vacuumed and dusted throughout the house. They emptied their suitcases in the bedroom and returned each item to its rightful place. Pictures went back on the walls. Laundry was washed, even the sheets on their bed and the bed in the guest room. Jennifer's nightgown was washed and folded. Fresh fruit sat in a beautiful bowl on the coffee table. Dried fruit was on a plate next to it.

Ingrid opened the door with a flourish. "Hi Jennifer, please come in." Then she spied Jennifer's muddy, wet-spotted pants and bare feet. "Goodness! Are you okay? What happened? Did you fall?"

Jennifer looked down at her pants. "I'm okay, my shoes are in the car. My feet are dirty. I shouldn't walk on the carpet."

Ingrid immediately handed her a pair of sandals sitting by the staircase. "Wear these…"

Donning the sandals, they went up the stairs and Jennifer headed to the bathroom, saying she should shower. Ingrid nodded, then went to her bedroom to find the new jogging suit and brand-new underwear Ingrid had bought from a discount store that morning. Jennifer was about to get undressed when Ingrid brought the clothes in, and when she saw the new underwear, she smiled broadly. It was like the biggest gift of her life.

"You are incredible. Thank you so much," Jennifer said.

This kindness, someone thinking about her needs, was unfamiliar to Jennifer. She sat on the edge of the tub holding the clothes in her hands. "You have such a beautiful heart."

Ingrid very quickly said, "I have done nothing compared to what you want to do for us."

A little while later, the aroma of food spread through the house. As soon as Jennifer walked in the kitchen, she said, "Smells good."

Rob grinned at her. "Ingrid's cooking is the best in town, and by the way, thank you so much for all of the fruits and vegetables. It will last a long time for us."

"You're welcome."

The table was set with their best china, Ingrid's mother's wedding present to them, only used on very special occasions. The first few times were when Rob and Ingrid found out they were pregnant, when they brought the baby home from the hospital, and when they closed on their house. Sandra's high school graduation and her acceptance into University figured into these special times as well.

Ingrid and Rob felt God had sent Jennifer to help them, and their faith had become tenfold, as had their optimism for their future.

Ingrid, while serving, turned to Jennifer with a smile. "What did you do today?"

"I painted."

"Oh? I didn't know you painted," Ingrid said.

"I stopped twenty-five years ago."

"What did you paint?"

"I don't know."

Ingrid sat down and waited a bit to continue the conversation. "You weren't looking at what you were painting?"

"My mind was with my brother, Justin. I was remembering him here in this home, eating, talking, or tripping with a glass of water. When the water spilled on the floor he would say, 'Osh, Jefe, osh.' Then he would sit next to the spill, and with his tiny hands, try to put the water back in the plastic cup."

After waiting several moments, Jennifer not saying anything further, Rob started to eat. Ingrid and Jennifer followed. Forks popped succulent bits of food into each of their mouths. All was silent except for the muffled sounds of chewing and the occasional sigh of satisfaction.

When dinner was finished, Rob and Ingrid shared a look before getting up to clean the table. Jennifer also rose and said, "Let me help."

Ingrid waved her back into her chair, saying, "Oh, please, sit. Rob and I have a team system for this chore." She smiled as Jennifer sat back down and silently watched as Rob took dishes from the table and handed them to Ingrid, who put them in the dishwasher.

Jennifer glanced to her right, and for the first time, noticed that the small porch behind the south side of the kitchen wall wasn't there anymore. That space was now part of the kitchen, with French doors leading to the backyard. She remembered her exhausted mother would wash their clothes in a sink on that porch. They had to go through the porch to open the single door to the backyard.

Ingrid opened the oven and took out a pound cake. "Do you care for coffee or tea with your cake?"

Jennifer had heard Ingrid's voice, but not the question. "You've done so much to the house. The kitchen looks great."

Rob said, "Wait 'til you see the garage."

"I remember the garage was just for my dad's gardening tools. It was full of junk."

Rob grinned. "All the more reason for you to see the garage."

Ingrid beamed at her husband and set the cake on the kitchen counter.

"Rob is the best husband one can ask for. He is so considerate and so loving. For a while there, as soon as he came home from work, he would work on the garage, as well as on the weekends. Bit by bit, the garage was transformed and became a private suite for visits from the in-laws. I am so lucky. He is my prince and my angel together in one. I love him so much."

Rob's cheeks reddened. "Honey, not now. You're making me embarrassed in front of Jennifer."

"But it's the truth!"

Jennifer watched their love toward each other amid the hardship they were experiencing. Sickness, no job, no money, and up to last night, the fear of losing their home, ready to sell all their furnishings. Jennifer thought of her mom and dad in this same kitchen and how unhappy her mom had been. Her dad was a very hardworking, simple man and was content with what he was doing. He expected dinner to be ready when he came home and the house clean. This exact same house, when she was growing up, was a sad home.

Her mind raced as she asked herself what the difference was between her parents and Rob and Ingrid, who were also high school sweethearts. Why were Rob and Ingrid so happy and still in love, and her mom was so sad all the time?

A deep memory surfaced with a swirl of emotions. The discussion her dad and mother had during one of the nights she was eavesdropping at the top of the stairs.

ಜ ಜ

"Marguerite, describe Honor killing to me," her father had asked her mother.

"What I understand about Honor killing is that they treat their girls different than their boys. As if girls are the property of the parents. And boys have total freedom."

"Is it like this everywhere in Iran?"

"Not at all. Iranians are highly educated people."

There was a pause, then her father asked, "Why is your family like that?"

Jennifer's mother took a deep breath. "Because my father, though he was born in Iran, his parents were from one of the very religious Arabic countries, and Honor killing is part of their culture."

"Do you know which Arabic country?"

"My mother told me, but I don't remember which one."

He continued asking her questions. "Have you met your grandparents?"

"Only once, when I was five years old."

"Does Iran have Honor killing?" Her father's voice had sounded insistent.

"It's possible. It's more of a custom in Arabic culture and in very religious families."

"So, on your father's side of the family, have they killed any girls in the name of Honor killing?"

"I have no knowledge about that. But they wouldn't hesitate to kill if their daughter ran away with a man or married a non-Muslim man." Tears slipped from the corners of her eyes, and Marguerite made no attempt to wipe them away from her face.

"Are you telling me that on your father's side of the family, they do not love the girls?" He raised his eyebrows.

"No, they absolutely love their girls and would die for them. But if a girl runs away or marries a non-Muslim man, the honor of the whole family is tainted. When honor is tainted, the shame on the family is unbearable, and they would be looked down upon by their peers. And if they have other children, no one will marry them." She explained to him, "They would be completely shunned by their community. In order to help restore honor in the family, a male in the family, a brother, father, or uncle, would kill the girl. By killing her, honor is restored in the family. The pain of the family's honor being tainted is viewed as so much more than the pain of killing their daughter. Honor in those families comes above love or the law." She rubbed the back of her neck.

It was silent for a while, until her father said, "It is a very sad culture."

Marguerite let out a hard sigh. "I know my escape brought much shame to my parents, and most likely to my sisters. I thought they wouldn't be able to find husbands because of me. I have so much guilt from hurting my family members. Although

I love you so much and would die for you, I am also in so much pain because of my actions and the unbearable pain I created for my entire family."

The doorbell interrupted their conversation. Marguerite took Christopher's hand and asked, "Are you expecting someone?" Christopher said no. He jumped to his feet and walked towards the door. Marguerite's eyes followed him. Mr. Newman, the neighbor from across the street, was at the door. Christopher opened it.

"Hello, Mr. Newman. Please come in. What can I do for you?"

"I just noticed your car lights are on, and I wanted to let you know."

"Thank you. You saved me from being late to work tomorrow."

Marguerite heard the conversation, went to the kitchen, grabbed the car keys, and handed them to Christopher. Mr. Newman and Christopher walked together towards the car. Christopher came back after a few minutes and sat next to Marguerite, took her hand in his and said,

"Honey, when we ran away, you were eighteen. In this country, eighteen-year-olds are adults and make decisions for themselves, for their own happiness. Any parent that forced their child under the age of eighteen into a marriage would go to prison. It is considered a crime. Even if a young girl is over 18, if she gets married because of the fear of her father, the father is no different than a pimp, yet they call it marriage. It doesn't make sense."

"We are lucky that my father didn't find out and that I don't have an older brother or uncle – and that my grandparents lived in the Middle East, not America. Otherwise, we would have been killed by one of them." She was taking shallow yet audible breaths.

"You were smart in not giving my name to your mother."

"I knew the culture. I knew we had to be careful so that no one in high school ever saw us together or knew we loved each other."

Christopher put his arm around Marguerite and kissed her neck. "Do you think your parents went to the high school to find out who I was?"

"I am sure my father asked every classmate of ours."

"I couldn't understand at the time, when we were planning to run away and you said to tell my classmates that I had been accepted to Stanford and was moving to Palo Alto to start summer courses."

The aroma of fresh baked cookies filled the room. Marguerite ran to the kitchen, saying to no one, "I hope they're not burned. I totally forgot about the cookies in the oven." When she came back, she sat next to Christopher, held his hand, and said, "Where were we?"

Christopher waited impatiently to continue the conversation. "Honey, we were talking about the time I told my classmates I was accepted to Stanford, and I was moving to Palo Alto."

Marguerite took a deep breath and continued.

"I was worried if you were the only one from the senior class that left town, my father might be suspicious. That he might find your parents and create problems for them or go through them to find us."

Her father sighed. "I remember when I told my classmates I was going to Stanford…a lot of them told me they were moving to different out-of-town universities, but they actually did."

"Yes, I remember. And that was lucky for us because my parents couldn't figure out that I ran away with you." She bit her nail.

"What would happen if a girl is raped?" her father asked.

"If parents find out that their daughter was raped, they kill her. I don't know the reason behind it, but I think it is because before marriage, a girl is not supposed to be touched by a man and must remain a virgin until she is married. So with a rape, the family honor is damaged. They kill the girl to restore the family honor."

Christopher leaned forward and asked, "What happens to the rapist?"

"The rapist might get a mild punishment but in most cases, nothing."

"The unfairness is extreme." He rocked his head back and forth in disbelief.

"Yes. The parents give their daughter the responsibility of protecting her virginity. And if it is taken by rape, then the girl must be punished because she didn't protect herself. And the punishment is death. I am so angry at this culture where girls have no voice, no choice, no power. They just have to obey their parents, who make their decisions, and they have to pretend to be happy about it." Her heart felt heavy with sorrow.

"Marguerite, you know how much I love you. We can put our energy into our kids. What we missed, our kids could have. I am so appreciative of my parents caring enough to pay for the girls' tuition to private school. At least we know they're getting a good education."

"I am grateful to your parents, too. I also love you very much, but sometimes the pain gets to me. I haven't seen my parents or siblings since we ran away. I miss them."

"I know that, but you know how dangerous it is for you to go see them."

"It is just too much pain."

෨ ෨

Ingrid and Rob shared a glance when they noticed Jennifer had gone silent. In a loud voice, Rob said, "Jennifer, I think you should park your car in the driveway."

Without saying anything, Jennifer got up.

"Jennifer, wait, you don't need to go out in the dark," Rob said. "Give me the key and I'll move the car."

Jennifer handed him the key and Rob went outside. When he returned, he was carrying the canvas and her red shoes. He put them on the empty chair next to Jennifer.

Ingrid set the cake on the table, along with a pot of chamomile tea. She tried to get a glimpse of Jennifer's painting as Rob started to cut the cake, but it was facing away from the table. In another moment, her curiosity took over. "Jennifer, may I look at what you painted today?"

Jennifer said, "Please, go ahead."

Ingrid carefully picked up the canvas and held it in both hands. It was a painting of their backyard in summertime, when the apple tree was full of apples. There were baby angels sitting on the apple tree's branches, hovering over apples on the ground, and flying above the apple tree.

"Jennifer, how did you come up with this idea?"

Jennifer's brows furrowed slightly. "What are you talking about?"

"What you painted."

"What did I paint?"

"You don't know?"

Jennifer shook her head, her gaze now on the back of the canvas.

Ingrid was beaming. "Look at it. It's amazing."

Ingrid held the painting in front of Jennifer, as Rob stepped closer, squinting at it. He suddenly smiled.

"Look at the angel sitting on the right side of the apple tree. His face is like the painting in the garage—"

"He's my brother, Justin," Jennifer said, looking at the painting. "I didn't know what I was painting. It was like someone else was moving my hands. Now I know it was my brother's spirit, wanting to let me know he is okay. Now I know he is okay. He is among the angels."

Rob pursed his lips and gave a quick look to Ingrid. "We have his picture in the garage."

Jennifer's gaze flicked from the painting to Rob's face, then to Ingrid's. They both nodded, then Ingrid said, "This is such a beautiful painting. Is the painting in the garage your work as well?"

Jennifer's gaze returned to her painting. "Probably. I was the only one in our family who loved to paint." She stood and asked Rob, "May I see the other painting?"

Rob nodded and turned to head for the garage. Ingrid quickly said, "Rob, you forgot to fix the light in the garage." Turning to Jennifer, she added, "Jennifer, it's dark in there... no electricity. You won't be able to see anything. How about tomorrow morning?"

Rob knew nothing was wrong with the light in the garage, but he didn't contradict Ingrid.

Jennifer sat back down, and they all tucked into their slices of pound cake. Looking closely at Jennifer, Rob now understood why Ingrid had stalled the trip to the garage until morning. She looked exhausted. She needed rest more than anything. All the paintings on the walls of the garage must be of Jennifer's family. The one of the young woman with such a sad face was most likely her mother. If Jennifer saw those paintings tonight, it might be too much for her in her current state of mind.

Rob smiled at Ingrid, reminded again of what a smart and compassionate woman she was and how lucky he was to have her in his life.

The next morning, Rob and Ingrid were still asleep when Jennifer opened the guest room door and very quietly went down the stairs. She quickly moved through the kitchen, opened the sliding glass door, and walked into the yard.

For the first time, she was looking at the apple tree without anxiety or being overwhelmed with sadness.

Taking a deep breath, she turned right and saw the side door to the garage. On each side of the door were very large windows. She went to the door and turned the handle. It was unlocked. She very quietly opened the door.

It was before sunrise and the room was very dimly lit from the opened door. She could tell that the wall facing the driveway was finished, with many pictures hanging on it. The windows on either side of the door had curtains, so she tentatively pulled on one until the gentle, pre-dawn light spilled into the room.

She noticed right away that this space was much different now than when it was her dad's tool storage. The garage was much larger than the one-car garage she remembered. The south side had been extended, adding enough space for a small kitchen with a table and two chairs. A full bath had also been added.

She opened the curtain covering the French doors that led from the cozy kitchen to the backyard, then sat on a chair, her elbows on the table, hands holding her chin. She looked out at a row of tulips in full bloom along the backyard's fence.

It came to her that her first drawing was of tulips that grew there years ago.

ဆ ဆ

When Jennifer was in the second grade, one night her father came home with two big bags. As soon as Angela saw her father carrying a bag in each hand, she ran to him, asking, "Dad, what do you have in the bags?"

Before her dad had the chance to answer her, Angela looked inside one of the bags and made a face. "Yuck."

Her dad said, "What do you mean, yuck? It's the tulip bulbs." Angela left and went upstairs, but Jennifer followed her dad into the yard. He said, "Tomorrow, we are going to plant all these in the yard and when spring comes, we are going to have beautiful tulips."

Marguerite stood next to the door to the backyard. "Christopher, where did you get so many bulbs? You must have paid a fortune for them."

"It was all free. Mrs. Martin decided to change the landscaping in her garden. I dug up all her plants and bulbs. She wanted them to be dumped, but I brought them here."

Without answering, Marguerite went inside.

The next day, Jennifer and her dad were in the backyard early in the morning. It was Sunday, so her dad was off work. He dug the holes for planting and Jennifer handed him the bulbs, until all the bulbs were planted along the bottom of the fence from east to west.

Jennifer was impatient for the tulips to grow. One day when she was in class, her teacher drew a picture of a tulip and she couldn't wait to talk about the bulbs she and her father had planted in their backyard.

Then finally, after a long and cold winter, spring arrived and their backyard looked different than years before, filled with blooming, colorful tulips.

This was the first time Jennifer sat with paper and pen to draw. She drew a picture of the tulips in her backyard. Then she took colored pencils and painted each tulip the same color they were in the garden. She was so excited to show the picture to her classmates.

She woke up early the next morning and got ready to go to school. She made sure she took the drawing of the backyard tulips with her.

At school, as she was showing her drawing to her classmates, one of the kids grabbed the drawing and said, "I'm going to tear this." At that moment, the teacher entered the room and heard Jennifer say, "Don't tear it, give it back to me."

The teacher got the drawing from the boy, glanced at it, then held it up to Jennifer with a big smile. "Jennifer, did you draw these tulips yourself?"

Her head down, Jennifer answered, "Yes."

Her teacher, still smiling, said, "Jennifer, you are very talented. Such a good job, bravo."

ಬಿ ಬಿ

Ingrid's voice calling for her brought Jennifer back from her childhood memories.

She came back to the house and was greeted by Rob, who had a cup of coffee in his hand for her.

Ingrid wore a worried look and asked Jennifer, "What happens if someone else wants the house?"

Jennifer went to her and took her hands. "Don't worry. I will buy the house. Just don't worry." She walked back to the table and retrieved the auction booklet from her purse.

Ingrid said, "Today is the auction day. What time does it start?"

"Do you mean the Philadelphia auction?" Jennifer scanned through the booklet.

Ingrid and Rob immediately cried out, "We lost the house! Philadelphia is a six- or seven-hour drive away. We would never get there in time. We lost the house—"

Jennifer waved her hand. "No, no! The auction for *this* house will be held in Pittsburg. Come here and let me show you." Jennifer turned the brochure so Rob and Ingrid could read it. Ingrid was already shedding tears and Rob had grabbed the back of a chair as though his legs might give out.

Jennifer pointed at the spot. "Look, look! Philadelphia is today and Erie is in two days in Pittsburg. This book has all the foreclosed houses in the whole state of Pennsylvania. It's not just for Erie."

Jennifer smiled as Rob peered at the brochure. Ingrid, holding her breath, gave a long sigh. "Oh, thank goodness." She smiled at Rob, giving his arm a gentle squeeze.

"Jennifer, since we are not going to the auction today, what do you want to do? My parents knew your parents and they are asking about you. Would it be okay if we go visit them?"

It took Jennifer a while to answer, and then, very politely, she said, "Not now, maybe later." She nodded her head toward the garage and added, "I saw the garage this morning. It is very pretty. Can I rent it from you?"

"It's yours," Ingrid responded.

Rob was quiet, listening. He thought about it and smiled. "It's very interesting that you would pay us rent money when you will be the owner."

Jennifer was very quick and assured with her response. "Yes, the title will be in my name; however, I will sign the deed back to you for the same price as the auction. You will repay me in installments. Part of the installment could be the rent from the garage. The garage is like a studio apartment, and until I figure out what I should do next in my life, it's a place to stay."

Jennifer took her canvas from the chair, then the red shoes, but dropped one. Ingrid was quick to pick it up and hand it to her.

"Jennifer, we need to go shopping." Jennifer didn't answer. Looking at the red shoes, Ingrid continued, "Wow. Those are fancy shoes. How can you wear such a high heel?" Jennifer still didn't answer.

Ingrid gently pushed on. "These shoes, why did you wear such a high heel while traveling?" Jennifer dropped onto the chair still holding the painting and her shoes. She went still and quiet. Tears gathered in her eyes.

"Oh my, Jennifer. I didn't mean to bring up sad memories. I am so sorry."

Jennifer dabbed at her tears with a napkin. "I bought these red shoes for my engagement party with Babak."

Rob came close to Ingrid, putting his arms around her, and softly said, "Jennifer, tell us more about Babak. How did you two meet?"

Jennifer leaned back in the chair, took a deep breath, and began the story of the first time they had met.

ಠಿ ಠಿ

The first time she met Babak was classic kismet. "Is this seat taken?" His voice was like warmed chocolate.

"I'm sorry, I forgot to take my jacket from the seat." She had offered a sincere smile.

"Are you an art major?" Jennifer asked.

"No, I took this class as one of my electives."

"I thought so," her statement made with such surety.

"Why is that?" His question held a hint of defiance.

"Because I didn't see you in any of the other art classes."

"You're very observant," Babak said.

Jennifer liked talking to him. "Only when I want to be."

He touched the crown of his cheek. "Are you Persian?"

Jennifer shook her head. "I'm half Persian."

"On your father's side?"

"No, my mother's. My dad is American."

"You look totally Persian." He smiled. Jennifer saw his dimples and thought he was gracefully good-looking.

Jennifer added, "I look more like my mom. My dad has blue eyes and blond hair." She asked about him, "You must be Persian."

"Yes, both my father and mother are Persian."

"I forgot to ask… What's your major?"

He flashed another brilliant smile. "Biology. My parents want me to be a doctor."

"What? Your parents want you to be a doctor, not you?"

"That's correct. I love art."

"Why don't you study art then?"

"Too complicated."

At this time, the teacher entered the class, and everyone became quiet.

There was something special between the two of them already. When their elbows touched while drawing, the tiny touch seemed to promise a long-lasting love story. Each could hear the other's breath, and soon their breathing became synchronized. They didn't want the class to end, and yet it had to.

Babak stowed his drawing supplies and said, "I am hungry. Let's have lunch."

She immediately blurted, "How about the café at College and Durant?"

"Great choice, we can walk there."

As they walked along, it seemed they went as slowly as possible so as to take longer to get to the café. They had to cross a street, and when a car didn't stop, Babak put his arm around Jennifer and pulled her away from the car. At that moment, they both felt an unrecognizable feeling – a kind of feeling they had never had before.

They sat across from each other in the café, and when they looked into each other's eyes, it was like they had known each other their entire lives. They both blushed and a few beads of sweat started to show on Babak's face. He quickly dabbed it off with a napkin.

"My name is Babak, what's your name?" His breath quickened.

"Jennifer."

"Jennifer is not a Persian name."

"I know, my family has no contact with other Persians." She shoved her hair back away from her face.

Babak leaned in closer to her. "You are lucky."

"Why am I lucky?" She toyed with her necklace.

"You are lucky because you're carrying less guilt."

"What do you mean?" Her sparkling eyes were wide open.

Babak rubbed his hands together. "In my family, they value boys so much more than girls. At the same time, they expect much more from them."

"What do they expect from you?" Her question seemed forward once it left her lips.

His expression and eyes were intense. "Don't get me wrong. I love my family, but I don't feel free with them. I am studying biology to become a doctor, while I love being an artist."

"Why don't you share your feelings with your parents?"

"It's not that simple. It's the culture; it's not my parents' fault. It is our family culture; no one lives for what their heart desires. They live based on how they want to be perceived by family and friends."

This sparked Jennifer's curiosity. "All Persians are like that?"

"Not all, however, my family and all of our friends live that way." He sighed and clasped his hands behind his back.

Jennifer flashed a big smile. "Babak, it seems like you can't be your true self in the company of your family and friends."

"Yes. That is one of the reasons I don't enjoy those elegant Persian parties. They are already calling me doctor, and I see how proud my dad and my mom are when a friend or relative calls me doctor. I have to smile while I get pinched in my stomach."

"Why do they call you doctor rather than by your name?"

A group of students entered the café and it became very noisy. It was almost impossible for Babak and Jennifer to hear each other, so they just stopped talking and gazed into each other's eyes.

When the café quieted down, Babak continued. "In Persian culture, education is very important. Being an MD has the highest prestige. After that is engineer, followed by a PhD degree. Calling a person 'doctor' or 'engineer' is a kind of appreciation for their education."

"It doesn't make sense. An accountant or an artist studies or works as much as an engineer or a doctor. Why do they have ranks in your family for different majors with different levels of respect?"

"Maybe it's based on their financial success to a degree. The pressure is unbelievable. For example, my aunt has seven children. All seven are doctors or engineers. I am sure among the seven, there should be at least one that prefers another major or maybe wants to be a musician, or an artist… but all followed the paths of being a doctor or engineer. And my aunt is the most respected mother in the family. Not to mention all these cousins also married doctors and engineers."

"What would happen if one of the kids didn't want to be a doctor or engineer?"

"She or he would be shamed by their siblings. Then there is the mother's guilt, feeling she must have done something wrong. There is so much pressure that getting the degree would be easier than dealing with the shame and the guilt."

"Wow. So, the mother's self-worth is connected to the children's education and their success in life."

A waiter came to their table, filled their water glasses, and asked if they wanted anything else. They each ordered another cappuccino.

Babak, tapping his finger on the table, said, "In our family culture, it's like a race between my family and my aunt and uncle's family. And it's all centered around the success of the children. My mother and my aunt don't have much education themselves. Their time is consumed by gossiping and boasting about their children's success."

"What is the role of a male in your family?"

"My father, the same as my uncle, are providers. And it seems they are in competition with each other for the bigger home, yacht, vacation home or more wealth."

"From what I'm hearing, it seems there is a competition going on among your family and relatives, and friends, on many levels. The men are competing against each other to create more wealth. The children are in competition for higher degrees. And the women's self-worth rides on the success of their husband's and children's higher education and wealth."

Jennifer was about to share with Babak how her mother had suffered because of the culture and not being able to be truthful to her parents. At the legal age of eighteen, her grandparents tried to force Jennifer's mother to marry a much older cousin. She ran away with Jennifer's father to escape the arranged marriage.

Yet Jennifer was conflicted; concerned because she didn't know how Babak would judge her if he found out her father was a garbage man, not a highly educated man like most Persians. So, she kept quiet.

Babak continued, "I'm impressed you got it so quickly. Now you understand how suffocating my life becomes when I must hide my true self and my desire in fear of shaming my parents. I am the only boy in the family and so much is expected of me."

"Do you have any sisters?"

"Yes, I have two sisters. I am the youngest sibling. One sister is an MD and the other is an engineer. Both are married." He gave her an appealing look.

"Which hospital does your sister work at?"

"She's not working. She is a stay-at-home mother." Babak leaned in closer.

"It must be very hard on her to study so much and stay home. That is a lot of sacrifice for the husband and children." She twirled her hair.

"They love each other very much."

"What does her husband do?"

Babak looked into Jennifer's eyes and smiled. "He is an engineer and has his own firm."

"Are your parents okay with your sister not working?"

Babak drew in a long breath. "Yes, the pressure of making money is only on the boys, not the girls. Girls must have higher education in order to end up with an educated, rich husband."

"You have a lot on your plate if your desire is art and you plan to become an MD and make a living as a doctor." She sighed.

"I know…" He blushed and looked in her eyes. "I'm so sorry, I just talked about myself."

She didn't mind. They left the café and walked toward the UC Berkeley entrance on Bancroft.

Babak slowed his pace to say, "I feel so comfortable talking to you. You're not like the girls in our family and our circle of friends. Is it possible to get your phone number and call you sometime?"

ಬಿ ಬಿ

Jennifer stopped talking and took a deep breath, staring at her empty coffee cup.

Ingrid and Rob were sitting, holding hands, anxious to know more about this love story. And why Jennifer still needed to say goodbye to Babak.

"Did you exchange phone numbers?" Ingrid asked.

"Yes..."

"How soon did you see him again?" Ingrid asked.

Jennifer took another deep breath, leaned back, and continued with her tale.

৪০ ৪০

Two days later, they were sitting in the same café, like two old friends that had known each other for years. Their body language showed how excited they were to see each other. Babak arrived first, and as soon as he saw Jennifer, he rose from his chair and walked to her with a big smile.

"I am so happy to see you again."

After ordering coffee and croissants, they sat side by side, then turned to be face to face. Babak started the conversation, saying, "I feel so comfortable talking to you. What I shared with you the other day was so hard, even admitting how much I love art. Today is your turn. I want to know about your interests."

"I truly love art and have chosen it as my major."

"What will you do after you finish school?" His mouth curved into a smile.

Jennifer blushed. "I want to be an art teacher. My best friend Elizabeth is also studying art. We both plan to be teachers," she answered.

"Have I met her?"

"I am sure you have. We always sit next to each other."

"Is she the blond gal with the short hair?" He tilted his head towards Jennifer.

"Yes, that's Elizabeth."

"She's pretty. How do you know each other?" he said curiously.

Jennifer took a deep breath. "I have known her since middle school, and we've been best friends since then."

"I know her boyfriend. He and I play basketball on the weekends sometimes with a bunch of other friends."

"Elizabeth sometimes complains that he plays too much basketball and doesn't study enough."

He couldn't help but ask, "Do you have a boyfriend?"

"No, I am not dating."

As soon as he heard this, Babak smiled and moved his hand to hold Jennifer's. She blushed but didn't pull away. Babak's touch made Jennifer's heart start pounding. After a few moments, she felt embarrassed and pulled her hand back.

Babak lost his smile, and asked, "Are you okay?"

"Yes, I am. How about you? Do you have a girlfriend?"

"My family has chosen a candidate for my marriage. But no, I am not dating, either."

"Tell me about the future wife your parents have chosen for you."

"She's pretty and studying to be an architect. She wears too much makeup. And each time that I've seen her, she's been dressed up like she's going to an Oscar party. She's perfect in many ways. But at the same time, she's not real. I don't know how she feels or what her true desires in life are."

"Ask her. She would let you know," Jennifer said.

"Impossible. If I wanted a trophy wife, she would be perfect. Not to mention her highly educated, rich family. My parents see her parents at their level. However, there is no connection between us.

That would be another disappointment for my parents, if I told them I don't want to marry her. I don't know how they would take it."

"I believe our parents are the older generation. They need to adapt to the younger generation, rather than trying to hold them down. Life is about moving forward. Nothing goes wrong when we follow our hearts. And if our parents don't like our choices, it's their journey to either change their beliefs and rules and be happy or stay in the sorrow and pain of losing control of their children."

Babak furrowed his brows. "So, in your opinion, I shouldn't worry about my parents. I should let them know I would like to be an artist, not a doctor, and tell them not to push me into an arranged marriage?"

"Being a pioneer always has its pluses and minuses. You must be ready, because being true to yourself will diminish your parents' hopes and dreams of approval and self-esteem for themselves among their family and friends. You being less than what they wanted will give them pain. Are you ready to witness that pain?"

"No, I prefer to suffer rather than see my parents be unhappy."

"Therefore, you are not ready to be a pioneer in change or breaking a culture that is not functioning anymore and is based on deception, control, and shame."

Elizabeth walked into the café and stood next to their table with a big smile. Jennifer introduced Elizabeth to Babak, who stood and took Elizabeth's hand in greeting.

Elizabeth gave a nod and looked at Jennifer. "See you at home. I'll leave you two love birds alone now." And she left.

Babak watched Elizabeth walk away, then turned to Jennifer. "I see my future. I will become a doctor, working a job I don't like. I'll be married to a Persian doll I don't love or connect with. And after having a few kids, my life will be about the children. I'll be living a life that is fake, empty, and sad. A life others would see as perfect."

Jennifer's eyes locked on his, her honesty coming alive. "That kind of life must be painful for the women as well, who marry someone without love. Let's imagine you, the doctor who has no connection with his wife at home, together only because of the children, or because you feel sorry for your wife. Would you end up searching for connections outside your marriage? Plus, after the kids are born, your wife may no longer look like the doll you married. Can you imagine *her* level of sacrifice in that kind of loveless marriage? She has given up everything: her job, her looks, her body, and in some cases, even her family and friends. And her reward becomes a cheating husband, or ending up divorced."

Babak leaned back. "You are going too deep. Tell me about your parents and how they ended up together."

Jennifer took a breath and said nothing. She didn't want to talk about her family. Instead, she looked at her watch and said, "It's getting late. I need to get going."

They left the café. As they walked along together, Jennifer's mind was preoccupied, remembering her parents' life. A fourth-grade experience now consumed her; Her friends talking about her father's job and laughing about him being a garbage man.

She was afraid that if Babak knew what her father did for a living, he would laugh at her. She was making the decision not to see Babak anymore when he took her hand in his and said, "Tomorrow, same place, same time?"

The touch of his hand melted her resistance. "Looking forward to it."

ॐ ॐ

The next day at breakfast, Rob and Ingrid were anxious to hear more about Jennifer and Babak. They were also curious to know why the phone call with her daughter disturbed her so much that she left San Francisco and drove to Erie in her nightgown and raincoat. They wondered why she needed to say goodbye to Babak, and if he was dead or alive. And what was the significance of the red high heeled shoes? They had so many questions.

Ingrid turned to Jennifer. "We would love to hear more about you and Babak. Is that possible for you to do? We care about what happened with the two of you."

Jennifer smiled at the kind couple who were a part of her life now and nodded, then took several sips of her coffee and continued with her story.

ॐ ॐ

"Tell me how a Persian girl ended up with an American boy. I want to know more about your family."

Jennifer swirled her spoon in her cappuccino and took a few deep breaths. "My parents went to the same high school. They liked each other very much. My mom hid this relationship from her parents, but she and my dad were always able to find a time and place to be together without her parents' knowledge."

"Wow. They were high school sweethearts. I'm surprised your grandparents allowed the marriage."

"They didn't. They didn't know anything about my dad. They didn't allow my mom to go to her prom and told her that night that they were planning a trip to Iran. One of my mom's cousins had asked for my mother's hand in marriage, and they had agreed. The cousin had a business in Iran and wanted to stay in Iran. So, my mom wouldn't be coming back with her parents to America."

"I can guess the cousin was fifteen or twenty years older."

"Yes, that is what I heard from my mom."

"Then what happened?"

Jennifer became quiet and remembered the many nights she sat at the top of the stairs, listening to her mom's heartbreak. Her shame, guilt, and pain. Watching her tears and sadness.

Babak repeated, "What happened next?"

She continued, "Marguerite, my mom, confronted her mother and told her she was in love with a boy at her high school and couldn't marry cousin Nassar. My grandmother told my mom that she must, that my mom didn't decide who she would marry, that her parents would decide for her. My mom said she loved him, but her mother countered by saying, 'A non-Muslim man? If your dad finds out, he will kill you. Don't you understand?'"

Jennifer suddenly pressed her lips tightly together and fell silent as the conversation continued in her mind. The memory of her mother's retelling of this terrible conversation to her father unwinding in seconds.

'You don't understand that you have to marry a Muslim. You have forgotten that you are to obey your parents and accept the decisions they make for you.'

'You want me to marry Nassar, who's seventeen years older than me and lives in Iran. I was seven years old when we came here; my life is here. How can you allow this marriage?'

'He is good for you. He is a good provider. We will go to Iran for visits, and Nassar and you can come to America to visit us.'

'I don't love him.'

'Love has nothing to do with it. The most important thing is that he is educated and a good provider. Your dad and his dad have engaged you. You know your dad; he prefers to die rather than to go back on his word.'

'I am your daughter; why do you want me to suffer?'

'That is the way it is. I married the same way; you will be fine. Don't tell me you are not a virgin. Has the boy touched you? If he has, your dad will kill him on the spot.'

'No, he hasn't touched me. I am a virgin.'

'Then what is the problem? Be happy. We will have the biggest and most elaborate wedding of all our family and friends.'

'I cannot do it. I am telling you. I will run away.'

'You know your dad and how religious he is. The idea of a non-Muslim man being with his daughter does not sit well with him. And if you run away with the boy, he will find you and he will kill both of you. Do it for me. Don't make me suffer because your dad takes your life and spends the rest of his in jail.'

Jennifer had abruptly stopped talking and now pressed her lips tightly together.

Babak took her hand. "What are you thinking, to be so quiet?"

"I was thinking about my parents."

"And so…"

"My mom gave up everything for love and ran away with my dad, and they started their lives together. But they were always in hiding for fear of my mother's father killing them."

"At least they lived with love," he said.

"Yes, that's true; they still love each other. However, my mom misses her parents and her siblings. It drove her into depression and has taken the joy out of her."

"I am sorry to hear that."

"My mom chose love, but she paid, and is *still* paying, a heavy price for it."

"I understand. It's the same in my family. If I don't marry the girl they have chosen for me, my parents will disown me. And the pain they would feel for having a son that didn't follow the family tradition would make them physically sick."

"It all stems from either not having self-worth or following a religious belief. Otherwise, they wouldn't care what others would say if children did not follow their parents' dreams. They should be happy for their children, even if their children's lives turn out different than what they had hoped for."

୫୦ ୫୦

Jennifer stopped talking, her head down, picking at her nails and biting her lip.

Rob, thinking Jennifer would feel more comfortable talking to Ingrid, got up from his chair and said, "I am going outside to wash my car."

Ingrid followed him to the door and gave him a kiss. "Thank you, dear. If you need help, let me know."

She came back to the kitchen, sat next to Jennifer, and took her hands. "Talk to me, please," Ingrid pleaded.

Jennifer finally whispered, "I feel lost. I worked nonstop. I gave up my joy and happiness to make sure my daughter would have freedom of choice in her marriage – and I feel I failed." The sadness, grief, and regret she felt showed on her face. She was looking down, seemingly at her toenails. The red color of her pedicure was almost half gone. Maybe she was thinking about missing her nail appointment.

Ingrid was anxious to find out what the phone call was about, as it seemed to be when Jennifer's troubles began. Plus, there might be a situation that needed tending to, and Jennifer was here, broken.

Ingrid broke the silence, quietly saying, "Let's go back to the phone call from your daughter."

Jennifer took a deep breath. "I knew Anita was calling me. No one else would call me that early in the morning. I picked up the phone – she was on the line. Then, my life didn't have meaning anymore."

"Why?" Ingrid pressed.

After a long, deep breath, Jennifer shook her head and said, "You won't understand."

"Try me…"

"I won't be able to have my daughter's engagement party at my home," she said.

"You left San Francisco…and drove here… because you can't have your daughter's engagement party at your home?"

"My life purpose was to give my daughter the freedom of choice, and now I took that freedom away from her." Jennifer curled her hands together in her lap.

"Tell me more…" Ingrid sat beside her and smiled gently.

"I didn't want money to stop my daughter's love and happiness the same way it stopped mine," Jennifer said, still whispering.

"Is that all?"

"I made sure she had higher education, financial security. I dreamed of her wedding, seeing her in her white dress. The white dress I never wore… the feeling I never felt… the white dress."

Ingrid's eyes went wide, her mouth open and her mind spinning. She couldn't believe this highly educated and wealthy woman could be so devastated about her daughter's engagement party.

Has she lost her mind? Ingrid felt her compassion for Jennifer shift. She thought about it. It was so easy for Jennifer to get the ten percent deposit for the auction. She drove a car worth more than their house, as Rob had pointed out. She had wealth when, in this economy, people were sleeping on the street, dying from hunger or lack of medical care. And this woman was upset about her daughter's lavish engagement party. Maybe sleeping one night on the streets might help her forget about all that.

Suddenly, Ingrid felt she could no longer hold her tongue with this stranger who crashed into their tragedy, promises of buying their house or not, and said, "Did you see the therapist I recommended?"

"No," Jennifer stated.

"Why not? You can't hide forever; you have a life in San Francisco. People are depending on you." Ingrid said in a serious voice, "I think you are depressed. You need to see a therapist to sort out your priorities in life."

"Do you know that every day I used to wake up with a vision? A vision so strong it made me work non-stop to achieve it."

"And what was the vision?"

"For my daughter to have the freedom of choice in her marriage."

Ingrid tried to get her to explain. "What does freedom of choice have to do with an engagement party at your home?"

Jennifer put her head on the table, then took a deep breath, and said, "I can't fix this. I can fix anything, but I can't fix this," she said, clearly upset.

Ingrid, still confused, opened her mouth with yet another question, but Jennifer suddenly stood up and hurried to the front door.

"Jennifer, where are you going?" Ingrid called after her.

She yelled back, "I am going to my car to look for my notebook."

Ingrid relaxed, deciding she'd done enough pursuing for the moment.

Rob was outside washing his car and noticed Jennifer walking swiftly towards her car. He called to her, "Jennifer, is everything okay?"

She didn't answer. Rob walked toward her and repeated, "Jennifer, are you okay?"

Jennifer waved an arm his way. "Yeah, I'm okay." And she sat down in her car.

After waiting more than half an hour, Ingrid went to look for Jennifer outside. She found her in her car, reading out of a notebook. Walking up to the car, she asked, "Are you okay?"

Jennifer didn't respond.

She tried again. "Jennifer, did you find what you were looking for?"

"I have written so many poems about our break-up…"

"Do you mean the breakup between you and Babak?"

"Yes."

"Let's go inside."

Ingrid opened the car door and took Jennifer's hand. The notebook fell from her lap and a few loose papers spread onto the ground. Ingrid picked them up. "Do you mind if I read these? Are they about Babak, too?"

"Yes…"

As soon as they were inside, Ingrid started to read.

Dance

It is a wedding.
Everyone is dancing.
I am also dancing.

I am dancing with you
In my mind.

Do you remember the time
I was in your arms?
We were dancing
In the middle of the crowd,
In a wedding
We crashed.

Everyone loved us.
They didn't care that
We didn't belong to
The groom or the bride's family.

We danced
And danced
The whole night.

Dog

I hear the neighbor's dog
Barking non-stop.

I should be worried.
What has disturbed the dog
In the middle of the night?

But my mind is with you,
Remembering the time
You were putting treats
On your dog's nose.

He was looking at you
With his big eyes,
Waiting for your signal
To catch the treat.

The dog is still barking,
And my mind is still with you.

Concert

Do you remember the time
We were at the concert?

Michael Bolton was singing,
But your lips were
Next to my ear.

I still remember
Every word you said.
I was so happy
And feeling light as a feather.

We were sitting so close,
On the same seat.
You held me with one hand,
Caressed me with the other.

I didn't want the night to end.
How happy and free we felt.

Michael Bolton is still singing his song,
But where are you
To hold me in your arms?

It wasn't fair to us
To break apart
While we were still in love.

FAE BIDGOLI

Birthday

Today is your birthday.
I have your favorite cake
On the table.

I put candles on it
And I will blow them out.

I will make a wish
For us to be together.

Do you remember
Your first birthday with me,
How happy we were,
How free we felt?

I looked for a gift
Many months in advance.
I couldn't find anything
That would express
My feelings.

Finally, I sat down,
Wrote the words
From my heart.

When you read the poem
I could see your smile,
And your tears
At the same time.

It is your birthday again
And I am blowing out the candles.
Happy birthday, my love.

Flight

I am sitting in the airport
Waiting for my flight,
To get away,
In search of a new life.

I want to start fresh
Without you haunting my mind.

I see couples walking,
Some holding hands,
Others who can't stand each other.

I wonder
If we were still together,
How tight
I would be holding your hand
In the airport.

Sun Has Left Me

Another Sunday
Sitting in a café,
Feeling lonely,
Drowning in my thoughts.
What else to do
Before the sun dies down?

But the sun never dies,
Even at night.
We can't see it
Because night
Has captured our eyes.

You were my sun.
Since we fell apart,
Night hasn't left my heart.

What should I do now?
Go home? See a movie?
It is too dark at home,
Even with the lights on,
Too lonely at the movies.

Restaurant

I am in our restaurant
Where we used to go for lunch.

Today is the last day
They are serving customers.

The doors will be closed.
My memories with you there
Will be locked inside.

I would eat there alone,
Hoping to feel the same as
When we had lunch together.

One more place
Is changing
And becoming unfamiliar
But not you, my love,
No matter how much I tried
To forget you.

Storm

It is after midnight.
I hear the storm outside.

It is pouring non-stop.
I can't sleep.

It is so lonely here,
Without you by my side.

I am wondering
If it is raining where you are.

I am sorry, my love,
Did I wake you?

Go back to sleep.
Don't let my thoughts
Keep you awake.

Rain

It is raining today
And it is such a gloomy day.

Since we have been apart,
I haven't enjoyed the rain at all.

We never used two umbrellas.
One was enough.

I enjoyed the rain
When you were at my side.

Every day the sun was shining,
Even a day like today.

Lonely Heart

A year has passed.
I know there is no future for us,
But my heart doesn't understand.

She speaks her own language,
Expresses herself with anguish.

She remembers every day and each event.
This shows how much she still cares.

She misses talking to you at night,
The weekends when you were around.

She is a lonely heart.

Two Birds

I woke at midnight.
I dreamt of you, again.

We were two birds flying,
Free of our boundaries.
No sense of our responsibilities,
Or rules of our religions,
Not even our family traditions.

Two birds,
Finally free—
To feel and to hold,
Each other for life.

Empty Seat

I sit in a restaurant,
A glass of wine in my hand.
But where are you
To share the drink with me?

I go to the movies,
Keep the seat next to me empty
And dream of the day
You'll sit next to me.

I go to the grocery store,
Walk down the aisles,
Buying food you like,
Wishing you will eat with me.

My life feels empty
Without your mysterious smile.

Friend's Wedding Anniversary

I came home
From a big party
Where my friend was celebrating
Her wedding anniversary.

I was sitting in a corner
Away from the guests
Thinking about
Our times together.

Maybe I should stop
Seeing my friends

Because I don't know
How long
I can pretend
I am okay,
Still alive
Without you
By my side.

Therapist

I am seeing a therapist
To help me move on.

Each session I cry a lot.
I blame myself
For hurting you so much
Because I didn't run away with you to Paris.
Please forgive me, my love.

I also blame
Our families
For the way they controlled our lives
And broke our hearts.

I am a mess, my love,
And I don't see any hope,
Even with therapy.

Spinster

It is my friend's wedding
And I am one of the bridesmaids,

I look at the bride and groom,
Remembering our own dreams.

I never did wear the white dress
Because no one could take your place.

I accept having become a spinster,
And I will stay alone
Until the day I become your bride.

Good Morning, Good Night

My minutes are occupied with you,
Except during meditation.

But even then
You sneak in
To show your love.

If I become a nun
And live my life for God,
Maybe then you will leave my heart.

Until then,
I wake up with your "Good morning"
And go to bed with your "Good night."

Ingrid lifted her head, her gaze lifting from the pile of papers on the kitchen table to Jennifer's face. "Wow, Jennifer, you two were in love! What happened?"

Jennifer leaned back, took a deep breath, and started to talk about the night she and Babak were supposed to be engaged.

৪০ ৪০

"Babak, are you sure your parents would be okay with announcing our engagement at the party?" Jennifer asked.

"Don't worry. They have seen you many times. They have even expressed that they like you."

"What about Noshin?"

"She doesn't matter. I love you."

"It's a Persian New Year party, right?"

"Yes."

"Is it formal?" she asked.

"Imagine the Oscars."

Jennifer panicked a little. "Oh, no. I need to buy a new dress."

"Don't worry. With what you have on now you will still be the prettiest girl at the party."

"Ha ha ha. You just love me."

Jennifer had decided to shop for a new dress, shoes, and accessories with her friend Elizabeth. She was worried about how she would look at the party, but at the same time, she was excited about her engagement announcement.

"Elizabeth, I am worried about the party. Babak was telling me that two hundred or more guests would be there and to imagine the Oscars."

"Don't worry, we'll find something nice for the occasion."

"I don't have much money to spare," she said sadly.

"It doesn't need to be expensive. It just needs to look good on you."

"I don't know..."

Elizabeth and Jennifer took the BART from Berkeley to San Francisco and got off at the Union Square station. They walked up the street and continued the upslope walk toward Union Square.

"Let's go to Macy's first," Jennifer suggested.

"How about Saks?" Jennifer smiled in agreement.

They entered Saks department store, took the escalator up, and started walking through the aisles, checking out the different designer dresses.

Elizabeth picked one out. "Jennifer, try this one."

"Let me see. Wow. Have you checked the price? I can't afford it."

They still hadn't found a dress, but when Jennifer saw a pair of red high-heel shoes, she knew they were meant for her.

After spending hours and hours at different department stores, Neiman Marcus, Nordstrom, and Macy's, Jennifer couldn't find a dress that fit her budget and the occasion. She became worried about how she would fit in with a highly educated, rich family like Babak's. She was feeling sorry for herself as they rode the BART back home.

The phone was ringing when she walked in. Babak was on the other line. "Jennifer, I forgot to mention that for Persian New Year, older people give presents to the younger people. I am one year older than you and I thought I would ask you what you would like."

Jennifer impulsively blurted out, "How about a new dress?" Shame immediately took her over; her cheeks became red and she wished she could take it back. One second was like hours until she said, "I am embarrassed now."

"Jennifer, what are you talking about? It is such a great idea. It takes the pressure off me of what to buy, plus it will be fun to go shopping together."

"I went to buy a dress with Elizabeth and couldn't decide what to buy. You said the party was going to be like the Oscars, and it scared me. I kept thinking that what I bought might not be good enough for the occasion. I ended up buying nothing."

The next day, Babak and Jennifer were holding hands and shopping together. Babak took her to a very fancy boutique in San Francisco and told her to choose whatever she liked.

"Babak, why this boutique? How do you know about this boutique?"

He replied, "This is where my mom and sisters shop."

She started browsing and checking out the clothes. She couldn't believe it. Every piece was priced at thousands of dollars. She took a deep breath and walked to Babak, taking his hand and whispering in his ear, "This place is too expensive. Maybe we should go to a department store."

"Honey, this is my present to you. You don't need to worry about the price."

She was hesitant. "But…"

"No but. Just choose the one you like and make me happy."

৪৩ ৪৩

Rob finished washing their car, came back to the kitchen, and said, "It's almost lunch time. How about I make barbecued chicken?"

Jennifer stopped talking and Ingrid quickly said, "Great idea! Marinated chicken is in the refrigerator."

Rob took out the chicken and some vegetables and headed for the backyard. Jennifer's eyes followed him.

Ingrid, impatiently waiting for Jennifer to continue, prompted her, "Go on, Jennifer. What happened next?"

Rather than answering, Jennifer took a water glass and began gently tapping it on the table. Ingrid tried to get her attention again. "Jennifer… Jennifer…"

But Jennifer's eyes were still locked on the French doors leading to the backyard, her mind far away, remembering her engagement night.

Ingrid got up from her chair and gently took the glass from Jennifer's hand. "Jennifer, please tell me about the engagement party. What happened there?"

Jennifer blinked several times, then turned to face Ingrid and continued with her story.

80 80

Jennifer was floating on clouds. Babak was holding her hand as they entered the great room. Music was playing and guests were dancing. Babak took her in his arms and they began dancing.

Jennifer leaned in close to whisper in Babak's ear, "Is Noshin here?"

"Yes," he answered.

"Which one is she?"

"The one with the yellow dress and hair to her shoulders."

"She's pretty," Jennifer remarked.

As soon as Noshin noticed Babak and Jennifer, she whispered something to the girl next to her.

Jennifer noticed that each time a guest was given the news, they would turn and look at her in surprise. At first, Jennifer didn't pay attention, then she became concerned. "Babak, look at the guests. They're talking about me."

"Of course they're talking about you, how pretty you are, how lucky I am to have you in my arms."

She decided she didn't care what everyone was thinking. She was in seventh heaven. His parents had received her very warmly. She didn't want the night to end. She had never felt happier and couldn't wait to wear her engagement ring. Everyone was having a good time.

It was after dinner that Babak's mother spoke to his father. They walked from the great room while Babak's mother gave Jennifer a look – it seemed she was sizing her up from head to toe. It wasn't an admiring look; rather, a look of disgust.

Jennifer couldn't understand what was going on. Suddenly, she felt in her gut that something was very wrong. She needed to breathe. The air had been sucked out of her. She let go of Babak's hand saying, "I'm going to the restroom to freshen up."

"Great. Good timing. When you come back, I'll be in the study talking to my parents about our engagement."

She went to the bathroom and looked in the mirror. She had thought maybe something was wrong with her hair or makeup. She checked her dress. She couldn't find anything different than when she entered the great room. She needed to think, to have a bit of time to herself. This lifestyle was so different from what she was used to. She went into the bathroom stall and sat on the toilet seat. The bathroom door opened and two girls, giggling madly, entered the bathroom.

"Can you imagine? Her father is a *garbage* man."

"How did you find out?"

"My father hired a private detective."

"Why?"

"You already know why. Babak is supposed to marry me. And ever since Jennifer pulled him away, he wasn't looking at me anymore. It was obvious he had changed his mind about me."

"It must be a mistake. Did you see the dress she was wearing? Her parents must be rich. It must be a mistake, and if you tell Babak or Babak's parents, it will come back to bite you. Keep it quiet until you are sure."

Noshin said, "We are sure. The private detective went to Pennsylvania and took a picture of her father on a garbage truck, and a picture of their home. It is so tiny. They are poor. She doesn't love Babak. She is faking it to get his money."

"Wow. What's next for you?"

"When Babak realizes Jennifer has been fooling him, he will leave her."

Jennifer started to shake and felt sick to her stomach. She wanted to leave the stall but had to wait until they left. One of the girls tried to push the stall door open and whispered, "Oh my. Someone is in there and heard everything."

"So what? It's the truth. Let's go use the other bathroom."

After they left, Jennifer hurried from the bathroom. She wanted to leave the party. She went to the study to stop Babak from telling his parents about the engagement. From his mother's look earlier, she knew they would be against it.

The study was on the opposite side of the great room; in between were the living room, dining room, family room, and kitchen. The study was in a very private part of the house. She finally reached the study and heard Babak's voice behind the door. Her heart went out to Babak and the way he was pleading to his father, "Dad, I don't want to marry her father, I want to marry *her*."

Another voice, Babak's father, spoke out. "You saw me. I liked her before I found out about her father being a garbage man. We would become the joke of our family and friends. The only son of mine, marrying the daughter of a garbage man. Unbelievable."

"She is perfect, even without wealthy parents. We are going to the same school. She needs to be admired for that. She is much better than a girl like Noshin, who has had everything handed to her."

"I have nothing against her. She is tall, pretty, polite, and I see how much she loves you. But your mother has a different point of view. She thinks she is faking it because of your money. She wants stability for her family, as well as herself."

Babak continued, "Dad, I love her, and I will marry her."

"Son, she fooled you. Think about it. You didn't know about her father; otherwise, a son of mine wouldn't date a girl like her."

"I knew about her father. But I am not marrying her father. I am marrying her."

"If you marry her, all of our family and friends will shame us."

"I can't understand why we have to live for others rather than ourselves."

"It is not that bad. Look at your mother and me, we didn't see each other until the day we got married. What is wrong with that?"

"What's wrong with that? Do you want me to tell you what's wrong? You are not happy with your marriage, and God knows who you loved before you got married. Tell me how many times you have cheated on Mom. You keep busy with work just to get away from her. You and Mom are practically roommates. You just want to prove you are richer than the rest of your family and friends."

His father said, "What's wrong with that? Your mom knows her role and I know mine."

Babak tried to convince his father. "How about an emotional connection? To feel love and be loved?"

"This is mumbo jumbo that started with American culture. Our culture is Iranian, not American, and we cannot mix it. What do you mean emotional connection? We are born to provide for and protect our children from harm. Babak, listen to me. I am telling you, she's trouble. You must stay away from her."

ॐ ॐ

Rob came back to the kitchen with plates of barbecued chicken and onion rings, bell peppers, and corn. The smell of fresh barbecue filled the kitchen and aroused Jennifer and Ingrid's appetites.

Ingrid got up to set the table. "God bless you, my love. I didn't know how hungry I was. You are one in a billion. Thank you. Thank you."

Rob replied, "All I have is for you, my blue iris."

Jennifer took in their love and passion toward one another and the harmony of their appreciation of each other. It seemed to her that the goal of each was to make the other's life more joyous. This relationship was so different from her parents' when they were living in the same house. Jennifer suddenly blurted out, "Family support."

Ingrid turned to Jennifer and smiled. "What do you mean... family support?"

"I have been comparing you two to my parents. So much similarity. However, the difference between my parents and you is the family support, which you two have and my mother didn't."

Ingrid quickly said, "Yes, I see what you mean. I'm so lucky. My parents live a few blocks from here. Rob's parents come from Philadelphia often to visit or we go there for the holidays. I can't imagine life without them."

Rob added, "Family is very important. However, for me, Ingrid is number one. As long as she's in my life, I can deal with anything else."

After a delicious lunch, Rob excused himself yet again. "I am going out to finally get my overdue haircut."

After he left, the room became quiet. Lunch had been cleaned up and put away, and the kitchen felt relaxed and homey. Ingrid touched Jennifer's arm. "So, did you leave the engagement party?" Her voice was soft and encouraging.

Jennifer's mind was entrenched in the haunting memory of her breakup with Babak. She glanced in the direction of Ingrid's voice, took a deep breath, and continued.

୫୦ ୫୦

"Babak, you know how much I love you. But we can't see each other anymore."

Babak was devastated. "I can't believe this; I am not my parents. You know how much I love you."

Jennifer continued, "Because I love you more than life, we cannot see each other anymore."

"I don't understand."

"If you marry me, your parents will be hurt and they will disown you. Then your education will stop."

He pleaded with her. "I promise you; I will continue my education."

"How?"

"I will get a job."

"You have never worked in your life. You will be miserable," Jennifer said.

"Let's get married. Both of us can work and go to school and make a life for ourselves."

Suddenly, Jennifer wasn't hearing Babak. Instead, she was hearing her mother's pain from being disowned by her parents. She took a long breath. "Babak, I can't do that to you. I can't make you suffer like my mother."

"What does your mother have to do with me?" he asked.

"I don't want you to end up like my mother, unhappy in spite of your love for me."

He looked deep into her eyes. "Jennifer, please don't do this to us."

They reached out to hug one another. They cried and kissed each other's tears.

Babak was also in a predicament. On one side was the love of his life, and on the other was his mother. His mother's life was about her children. It was the children's job to act and behave a certain way so she felt fulfilled and important. Manipulation and control were part of his mother's nurturing. She had instilled enough guilt to ensure Babak would follow her wishes. And Jennifer understood that.

"Babak, you know you can't marry me. How would you feel if something happened to your mother? She would feel so much shame; she would isolate herself from all her family and friends. She would have to hear so much gossip about our marriage it would affect her physical and emotional well-being."

"I hate this cultural cruelty and the pressure of keeping up with the Joneses."

Jennifer looked at him. "Do you see? We don't have a choice."

"We can get married. We don't have to tell them," Babak said.

"They would find out. It's just not possible."

"The heartbreak could kill us."

Together, they accepted their fate. They held each other for hours filled with gentle, soft kisses and stroking one another's face and hair. Ultimately, their bodies became one.

ೞ ೞ

"Jennifer, did you see Babak again?" Ingrid asked.

"Yes." Jennifer answered through a haze. Ingrid wasn't sure if Jennifer was answering her question or one from the depths of her memory.

She asked again. "Jennifer, did you see Babak again?"

"Yes."

She knew she had to press her to get more of the story. "Tell me about it. How and when did you see him again?"

Calmly, without any resistance, Jennifer resumed her story.

દ૦ દ૦

"Elizabeth, leave me alone."

"He's on the phone again. He wants to talk to you."

While Jennifer was desperate to see Babak and hear his voice, yearning to have a moment with him, the love she had for him was so strong that she couldn't bear it if he were to become like her mother. So, her mother's pain stopped her from running to the phone.

Elizabeth was on the phone with Babak. "Babak, I am so sorry for what happened to both of you. You two were so perfect for each other." She decided to tell him the truth. "She is not going to school anymore. She just stays in bed, crying."

"Why doesn't she want to talk to me?" he asked.

"She thinks you will be better off without her."

"How could I convince her to talk to me?"

Elizabeth told him, "She is set in her mind. I've tried over and over to get her to pick up the phone. She won't listen to me."

"I am coming over. Please, don't tell her."

Elizabeth hung up, grabbed a chair, took it to Jennifer's bedroom, and sat down on it next to her bed.

"Jennifer, Babak truly loves you. He is willing to give up everything in his life in order to be with you. Don't throw that away."

120

"You don't understand."

"What don't I understand? Love like this doesn't come easily. You may never fall in love again if you lose Babak," Elizabeth said.

"He's better off without me. He'll continue his education, become a doctor, marry Noshin, and be able to keep the same lifestyle."

"He loves *you*. Not Noshin. He won't be happy without you," she tried to convince her.

"If I run away with him, he will be disowned by his family. Then he has to quit his schooling. He will become like my mother. Sad and depressed, despite his love for me."

Elizabeth continued, "No two circumstances are the same. The way a woman deals with emotion is different than a man. He may not become depressed. He may even feel freedom about leaving that culture."

Jennifer was stubborn. "You haven't witnessed my mother's depression. You don't know the depths of her sadness of missing her parents and siblings."

"Girl, you need to talk to a therapist to sort all this out. You're making decisions about your future and the love of your life based on your mother's pain."

"No. I am making decisions because of my unconditional love for Babak."

Elizabeth was running out of steam. "Babak can make his own decisions. And he has chosen you over his parents' wishes. Otherwise, he wouldn't be knocking at your door so many times. Or calling over and over with the hope of getting any response from you."

During this deep discussion, the doorbell rang. Elizabeth knew it must be Babak and she ran to the door, ignoring Jennifer's orders.

"If it's Babak, tell him I'm not home."

Elizabeth opened the door and told Babak, "She's in the bedroom."

As soon as Babak reached her room, they were in each other's arms, kissing.

Jennifer was the one to break it up. "Babak, wait… wait."

"Don't talk," he murmured. "I miss you so much."

For hours they held each other in bed. Then finally, they started to get hungry and decided to go out to eat. Babak drove them to Solano Avenue.

Jennifer turned to him. "Babak, why Solano Avenue?"

"There's a Persian restaurant I want to take you to. Have you been to a Persian restaurant before?"

"No, I haven't. How about you?"

"I have been to many Persian restaurants. Wait until you try their kebabs. They are so yummy."

She told him, "I haven't eaten for the last few days."

"I'm glad I took the chance and came over."

They entered the restaurant and it seemed the owner knew Babak, from his warm welcome. They chose a quiet corner table. As soon as they sat, the waiter brought them fresh hot bread, cheese, and some scallions, turnips, basil, and mint. Babak took a piece of bread and put cheese on top, along with basil and mint. He rolled it up like a sandwich and gave it to Jennifer.

She was impressed. "Wow. This is delicious. What kind of cheese is this?"

"Persians use only feta cheese, which is similar to French feta."

Babak ordered almost everything on the menu, then said, "We will sit here and eat all the food I ordered until I convince you to come with me to Paris."

"What do you mean?" Jennifer asked.

"I have reserved two tickets for us to fly to Paris a week from today."

"How did you convince your parents?"

"I told them that if they wanted me to give you up, I needed to go to another country and university. They suggested Paris."

"Do they know anyone there? Do you have family there?"

"No, there is no family or anyone we know there. In Persian culture, to study in Paris has more prestige."

"Again, if I go with you to Paris and your parents find out, you will be disowned, and it will be a much bigger pain for your parents because you lied to them."

He tried to reason with her. "Jennifer, I am trying to find a solution. This way, we can continue our education and by the time they figure it out, we'll have graduated."

From their table, they could see the street, and at this moment, Jennifer noticed an ambulance parked across the street. Suddenly, she saw herself standing at her childhood bedroom window, watching three men load her mother into the ambulance. Her mother's pain came back to her heart full force and she said, "Babak, I cannot do that to you."

"What do you mean?"

"I cannot run away with you to Paris," she stated firmly.

"Why can't you?"

"They found out who my father is and where my parents live. They can easily check on you in Paris."

"If you are worried about Noshin and her parents, they are not our friends anymore. They are the ones who told my parents about your family."

"I know."

He was surprised by what she said. "How did you find out?"

"That night, when you went to the study to talk to your parents about our engagement, I went to the bathroom to freshen up. I was in a bathroom stall when Noshin and another girl came in, giggling and talking about her parents hiring a private detective to spy on my family. And how they took pictures of our home and my dad on the garbage truck."

He was infuriated. "They are such nosey people. I'm so sorry that happened. It must have been so painful for you. What did you do after hearing that?"

"I waited until they left, and then came to find you, to stop you from talking to your parents about the engagement. I knew they wouldn't approve of us once they found out. I heard your father trying to convince you to give up on me and you were pleading with him. My heart went to you, but then I realized it was not my place to stay at the party any longer."

She continued. "While I was leaving, it seemed like everyone knew about my life from the way they looked at me, sizing me up. I couldn't breathe. In a mere thirty minutes, I went from dancing in your arms and feeling the happiest I've ever felt in my life, to suddenly being back in fourth grade, feeling small, hopeless, sad....

"I was about to open the door to leave the house when I heard your mother very loudly say, 'I am so glad the truth came out, and this imposter is out of my son's life. As you all see, she was such a good actress. We even believed she was in love with Babak.'

"I closed the door behind me but couldn't move. I sat behind the door. I wanted to die. The shame was overwhelming. The windows over the door were open and I could hear them. 'There must be a mistake. The daughter of a garbage man cannot wear a dress like the one she was wearing. Plus, she is pretty, well mannered, going to UC Berkeley, and your son loves her. There must be a mistake.'

"Your mother said, 'There is no mistake. God knows how much money my son has given her and her family. And, most likely, my son bought the dress for her as well.'

"Then Noshin stepped in. 'We have pictures of her father on the garbage truck and of their tiny home.' Then many voices expressed sorrow for your mother. Things like: 'She must be a prostitute.' And 'maybe your son is not the only one.' 'Has anyone checked to see if she really is a student at UC Berkeley? Maybe she is pretending that as well.' One thanked Noshin's parents for protecting you and your parents from my awful scam.

"They were still talking when I was finally able to walk away. I knew you would follow me, but I wanted to be alone. I hid in a small alley nearby until I saw you drive away. Then I walked until I found a phone booth to call Elizabeth and ask her for help."

He was deeply saddened by what he heard. "I am so sorry. You didn't deserve that." Babak reached out and took Jennifer's hand, pulling her toward him and held her close.

Jennifer said, "You said Noshin and her family aren't your family's friends anymore. What happened?"

"When I came out of the study that night, I looked for you. I asked everyone if they had seen you. Then I noticed a large crowd of people near the entry door in a big circle around my mother. Everyone was giving her some sort of advice. As soon as she saw me, she took my hand and said, 'We need to thank Mr. and Mrs. Rahmani for protecting us.'

"I said, 'What do you mean? Where is Jennifer?'

"'Jennifer is gone.'

"'What do you mean she's gone?'

"'Did your dad talk to you about her?'

"'Yes. So what?'

"'What do you mean, so what?'

"I looked into her eyes and said, 'I am going to marry her.' As soon as I said that, my mother fainted in front of everyone. One of the guests grabbed her and eased her to the floor. At this point, Noshin's mother stepped in and said, 'We love you and your family. We know you didn't know Jennifer's father is a garbage man. We needed to step in to help your family.'

"My blood was boiling like hell. I shouted; asking if she thought I would give you up and marry her daughter. I kept shouting that I wouldn't marry Noshin if she was the last girl in the entire world, to get out and never come back, that no one had asked for her help and to just get out.

"They left shortly after, with my mother still on the floor being tended by one of my parents' doctor friends, along with my sister. As soon as I knew she didn't have a heart attack, I started looking for you in my car."

Jennifer shook her head and sighed. "How is your mom now?"

"She was sick up until a few days ago when I said I would go to Paris. Of course, they think I'm going alone."

"Her sickness is real. Her whole identity is tied to her kids, especially her son. And if you marry me, which in her eyes is blasphemy, it's like her hopes and dreams are shattered. Not only will she be depressed, she may also become physically sick."

"You're right," Babak conceded. "At first I thought she was faking it. Then when the doctor showed me the test results, I realized she was sick."

"Your mother would go to any extreme to stop us from being together."

"I know that now. Finally, I figured it out. The only way was for us to live in a foreign country, and now, I also understand why you didn't want to see me anymore. Even while you were telling me you loved me more than life. And because you loved me,

126

we needed to stop seeing each other." He desperately wanted to change her mind. "But my dearest, Paris gives us the opportunity to be together. And my parents feel I am following their wishes. What they don't know won't hurt them."

By the end of the night, they were talking non-stop about what they would do in Paris, which art galleries and museums they would see.

The next several days passed in the blink of an eye. Jennifer was busy with packing and talking to her parents for hours and hours about her trip to Paris.

She said into the phone, "Mom, don't worry. I will come to visit you."

"Why Paris? Finish your bachelor's degree at UC Berkeley, then go to Paris for a master's degree."

"Mom, Babak is going there to study, and I will go with him."

"Honey, I am scared you won't finish your schooling and you'll end up having kids and repeating my life."

Jennifer tried to calm her fears. "Don't worry. You know how important school is to me. And no matter where I am, I will finish my degree."

"I know you have the intention of going to school there; however, with a move like that, your path may change. And God knows what changes life could bring, even with all of your intentions of getting a degree."

"Don't worry. Everything will be fine."

"How are you going to manage financially? Where will you live? How will you pay for your tuition there?"

"Babak is taking care of everything."

"Since you finished high school, you have been on your own with your student loans and part-time jobs. You have been independent. This move makes you dependent on Babak. I am so scared you will repeat my life of dependency. Even though I was in love with your dad, part of me lost its freedom, and my soul is yearning for that freedom." Her mother paused before continuing, "The best kind of love is when two people are independent of each other and yet inter-dependent."

"Mom, with the way Babak and I love each other, we will survive any hardship we may face in Paris."

"Honey, I thought the same when I ran away with your father."

"Mom, don't worry."

"At least talk to your school to get permission for a one semester leave of absence; in case things don't work out in Paris and you come back. Then you can continue your education here."

"Great idea. I'll do that."

Since Babak knew his whole family would be at the airport to say goodbye, he bought Jennifer's ticket for a different flight — five hours after Babak's.

ɞ ɞ

Jennifer stopped talking and had a faraway look in her eyes. Ingrid put her hand on top of Jennifer's and gave it a soft squeeze. "Oh my…I hope you went to Paris with him."

"No, I didn't."

Rob gave a 'halloo' call as he came through the front door, back from his haircut. Ingrid ran to him and ruffled his hair. "You arc so handsome. Great haircut."

Rob took her in his arms for a huge hug and he said softly in her ear, "It seems you two are having a deep discussion. I'm going to watch television in the bedroom. I was listening to the news on the way home and it seems Obama is ahead in the polls. I want this man to get elected." He gave her a kiss and as he went up the stairs, chanted, "We need change. We need change."

Ingrid smiled and headed back to the kitchen, saying to no one in particular, "Rob's right. All the money we've spent on the Iraqi war... money that would have been more than enough to bail all of us out that are losing our homes. Money that could have created so many jobs. Rather than closing factories, more factories could have been opened. What was the benefit of that war for people like us?"

Rob apparently heard her and called down the stairs, "Honey, they don't care about people like us."

Jennifer was quiet and wanted to change the subject. "How about a cup of coffee? Let's go to a café."

Ingrid waved her hands dismissively. "No way. I will brew us a pot of coffee and you'll tell me why you didn't go to Paris with Babak."

Jennifer licked her lips and nodded, then began recounting her story.

 හ හ

There was a knock at the door. It was Babak. Instantly Jennifer asked if the Paris trip had been cancelled and he smiled and said, "I just missed you. I wanted to see you before our trip tomorrow." And he picked her up and walked to the bedroom.

They could not wait to be in Paris and be free to be together every day and night. To share the same bed and fall asleep in each other's arms. Their hopes and dreams extended to future children.

"How many children do you wish to have?" Babak had asked.

"Only one. Hopefully a girl. How about you?"

"I want a girl, as well. Also, a boy. Therefore, two. No, two is not enough. How about ten?" He chuckled.

"Ten? Can you imagine almost ten years of being pregnant, ten or twenty years of breastfeeding? Wow. Impossible. I don't understand how my great grandmother gave birth to eleven kids, and she was all smiles all the time, or so I heard."

"Which great grandmother?" He winked at her.

"On my mother's side. Now I understand why my grandmother married a man from an Arabic country… because they had so many children they couldn't wait for a nice suitor, so they would marry their daughters to the first man who showed up and asked."

Babak rubbed Jennifer's shoulders and kissed her on the neck. "Okay. Okay. I was kidding. You want one, then we'll have one!"

"What happens if the first child is a boy and I want a girl?"

"Then we will have two."

Jennifer tucked a lock of hair behind her ear. She disagreed. "No. Only one. Boy or girl, doesn't matter."

"Oh, my beautiful girl, I can't wait for tomorrow when we are headed to Paris."

Jennifer's lips turned up into a smile. "Have you packed?"

"Yes…well, my mom did most of the packing. It will be exciting starting our lives together away from all the family pressure."

"Convincing my mother that going to Paris wouldn't stop my education was difficult. She still thinks I am making a big mistake."

After hours and hours of holding each other in bed, kissing, caressing, making love, and talking, Babak flipped to the edge of the bed and sat up in a panic. "What time is it?"

"Nine," she answered.

"Oh my, I need to run. My parents have a goodbye party planned for me. Let me call to let them know I'm running late."

Jennifer handed the phone to Babak, while lying next to him and kissing his face.

Babak dialed, reaching his mother. "Hi, Mom."

"Where are you? Everyone is asking about you."

"Sorry. I'm on my way."

"What is more important than your own goodbye party?"

"I said I'm on my way," he said.

"Please hurry up. Your uncle Bijan and your cousin Ardashir are here."

"I thought they were in Canada."

"Yes, they are living in Canada."

"Are they visiting us?"

"As you know, Ardashir's dream was to come to America and to go to University here. At least to one of the UC's. Although his dad was aiming for Harvard, Princeton or Stanford."

"I know all about this. Ardashir's scores were low and he couldn't get accepted to any of those universities. I know the whole drama about his education. But what does this have to do with me and the party?"

"Uncle Bijan and Ardashir are going to Paris with you. Uncle Bijan will stay there for a couple of months until you two are settled. You know Uncle Bijan got his degree in Paris and is very familiar with the city and the universities there."

Babak was panicking. "Why are you telling me this now and not sooner?"

"I wanted to surprise you. It will be much easier on you with him along."

"You should've consulted with me before trying to convince them to go with me to Paris."

"It was their decision."

"I know the decision was theirs. However, I am one hundred percent sure you had to do a lot of convincing. I bet you're even paying for all of Ardashir's expenses in Paris."

"What is wrong with me helping my nephew?"

"I'm not coming to the party. Let the guests know."

"I thought you would be excited about them coming along."

"You wanted someone to spy on me. I'm not going to Paris."

"Why are you so upset?"

"I'm not going to Paris. I want to see if I don't go to Paris, whether Uncle Bijan and Ardashir still go." His hands clenched into fists.

His mother started crying, begging her son to come to the party and go to Paris. "Please come over. This is so stressful for me. I am about to faint again."

He hung up on her.

Jennifer had listened to the whole conversation. They held each other in silence. After a while, Babak said, "Jennifer, let's stick to the plan."

"How can we? You will be disowned."

"Ardarshir is young and understands love and the family culture. He won't say anything."

"But your uncle Bijan would."

Babak pulled Jennifer closer to him and held her tight. "I will try to convince him not to say anything."

Jennifer was unsure about everything. "Your uncle had the same upbringing as your mother; he would be against you being involved with me."

"You're right. He's worse than my mom," he said sadly. "Okay, I won't go."

"Even if you stay here, they'll follow you to see if you're with me." Memories of the Persian new year party flashed across her mind.

Babak let out a heavy sigh. "So what? Let them follow us. Let them disown me. I will take care of myself. I would prefer to work non-stop if it meant I could come home and see your beautiful face and have your head on my chest when I fall asleep."

"What about your mom?" Her eyes welled up.

Babak was anguished. "What about her? If I must give up one of you, I'd rather give up my mother."

"How would you feel if she became sick or died from the heartbreak of her son going against her wishes?"

"I don't want to go there."

Jennifer was fighting back tears. "You need to face it. Your mom's identity and self-esteem are linked to your education and who you marry."

Babak's jaw trembled with rage. "I feel suffocated with this Persian style of living. It's all pretend, like the self doesn't exist." He looked at her and said, "Sorry, honey, such a bummer on our happy life together in Paris. We can still be happy living here though."

"I can't..." she said, defeated.

"What do you mean?" His temples pounded with each beat of his heart.

Jennifer searched for words. In the span of a few seconds, her childhood and seventeen years of living with her parents danced before her eyes and she searched for her mother's smile. Her mother's joy. For one moment of happiness. But she couldn't find one in all her memories. Her mother's life had been consumed with guilt, shame, sadness, and endlessly being homesick, missing her parents and siblings terribly, despite her love for her husband and children.

Jennifer decided that if, amidst her memories of her mother, she could find some joyous or happy times, she would say yes to Babak. Whether to go to Paris or stay in Berkeley and start their life together.

Her mind raced through memories of her mother's life, which was consumed with house chores – washing dishes, cooking, washing clothes – non-stop. There wasn't a friend or family gathering at their home that she could remember.

Babak searched her expression for clues, then said, "Tell me why you can't."

Jennifer sighed softly and looked him in the eyes. "Because I love you too much. And I can't burden you with the pain and the guilt if something were to happen to your mom."

"Don't say that."

"You need to go to Paris. I am not going with you. The distance will be good for us, and hopefully we'll heal."

"What are you talking about?"

She didn't want to say it, but she had to. "I think this is the end for us. Your family will never change their opinion about me."

Babak couldn't believe what she just said. "You're sacrificing your own happiness for my mother's control over me."

"I'm sacrificing my own happiness for you, my darling. You haven't watched my mother slowly dying from the guilt she felt when she ran away with my father. I don't want you to experience the same guilt and sadness."

No matter how much Babak tried to convince her to join him in Paris, Jennifer's mind was made up. Through the night, they held each other in bed, kissing, caressing, and making love. When sunrise came, it was time to say goodbye.

Babak had decided to take the flight to Paris.

Elizabeth had spent the night with her boyfriend. She came home that morning and saw Jennifer in bed, her ticket to Paris on the coffee table in the living room. She picked up the ticket and walked into Jennifer's bedroom. "Why aren't you ready? It's about time to take you to the airport. Hurry up."

"I'm not going. His parents are sending his uncle and his cousin to Paris as chaperones to make sure I won't be joining Babak."

"What did Babak have to say about this?"

"He still wanted me to go with him."

Elizabeth asked, "So why aren't you?"

"His family will never approve of me."

"So what? Babak is not his family."

"I know, but it's complicated."

"There is no complication. You two are in love. Follow your heart and don't make it so difficult for Babak to be with you," she said, a little annoyed that she had to keep having the same conversation with her.

"Running away together because of love, without the approval of family, is not enough for a happy life."

"It should be!"

"You don't have a family like Babak's. There is so much control, shame, and blame woven into the upbringing of their children."

"But Babak has chosen you."

"Choosing me without his parents' approval wouldn't give him the happy life he deserves."

Elizabeth kept trying. "You're making the biggest mistake of your life. Someday you will wake up and realize you let go of the most precious person in your life. And all because of the possibility that Babak may not be fully happy without the approval of his parents."

Jennifer started crying. "I want to go to Paris. But I can't."

She tried one last time. "Listen to me. We have been friends since middle school. Just trust me and let me give you a ride to the airport." Elizabeth took Jennifer's hands and tried to pull her out of bed. Then, in a commanding voice, she said, "Get dressed! I'm taking you to the airport."

"Too late. He already left. Even if I went to Paris, I have no way to contact him."

"I give up…" Elizabeth threw her arms up in despair and left Jennifer's bedroom.

ॐ ॐ

Jennifer went silent, looking very miserable. Ingrid's eyes were wide and she was biting her lip. She took Jennifer's hands into hers and slowly shook her head. "I am so sorry, Jennifer. I am just so sorry."

The next day, Ingrid and Rob welcomed Jennifer to the kitchen with a glass of freshly squeezed orange juice, then Rob started making his famous artichoke and cheese omelets. Ingrid continued reading another page of those that fell from Jennifer's notebook.

She paused and nodded encouragingly to Jennifer. "Did you see Babak again after he moved to Paris?"

Jennifer looked down before replying. "I need a cup of coffee first."

The omelets were ready, and Rob set out cups of coffee. All three started eating the delicious egg concoction.

"Wow... such a yummy omelet," Jennifer said after downing the last bite on her plate.

Ingrid beamed at her husband. "There's nothing Rob can't do. He's not only my husband and best friend; he's also my cook, handyman, gardener, chauffer, grocery shopper, and much more. I'm so lucky."

"I'm the lucky one, my blue iris," Rob said and winked at her.

After breakfast had been cleared away and a second cup of coffee poured, Ingrid asked again, "Did you see Babak again, after he moved to Paris?"

Jennifer took a sip of her coffee. "Yes. I saw him one more time."

Ingrid couldn't contain her curiosity. "When was that?"

"I was pregnant with Anita. I saw him from a distance."

"Are you referring to this poem?" Ingrid pointed to one of the papers on the table.

"Yes."

Saw You

I saw you today.
You were walking
Next to the bank.
I was driving in my car,
And stopped,
Rolled down the window
To scream your name,
But the shock of seeing you
Made me paralyzed,
Locked my mouth.

I heard the sound of horns
From cars behind me,
But I couldn't
Continue driving.

You didn't see me.
You walked away.

I am still in the car,
Lost in my feelings.

Jennifer's memory of that day came back to her.

"Elizabeth, I saw him. He's back from Paris. I was in my car. He was crossing the street."

"You didn't stop the car and follow him?"

"By the time I parked and started looking for him, he was gone."

"Let's call his home and talk to him."

⁊ ⁊

Ingrid tapped Jennifer's shoulder. "Jennifer... Jennifer?"

"Sorry, what did you ask?"

She repeated, "Did you talk to Babak?"

"Elizabeth and I tried the home number, but it was changed."

"How about going to their home and knocking on the door?"

"We did that. We went to Babak's home. The butler said he had left for Paris and practically threw us out on the street. Told us never to come back again."

"So, that was the last time you saw him?"

"Yes."

Jennifer was quiet, deep in thought again. Ingrid took her hand and looked into her eyes. "Jennifer, Anita called you on the phone. What did she say?"

Jennifer blinked several times, then said, "Ingrid, tomorrow is the auction day."

"Oh my, you're right. I hope nothing goes wrong."

Rob was making another pot of coffee and when he heard Jennifer mention the auction day, he came back to the table, stood behind Ingrid's chair, and put his hands on Ingrid's shoulders. Looking at Jennifer, he asked, "Can anything go wrong with the bidding?"

"Nothing will go wrong... and I will have the winning bid," Jennifer said.

"We are so much luckier than our neighbors. Yesterday, I met some of them on the street. They are in the same situation we were," Ingrid said.

Jennifer looked up from her coffee with a jerk. "Which neighbors are you talking about?"

"On our street there are five homes, including ours. The street behind us has two homes, and the street before ours has three homes."

Jennifer was curious. "What do you know about those neighbors? Can you show me their addresses in the auction booklet?"

Ingrid looked at the auction booklet of properties and showed Jennifer each house. Jennifer then marked each address with an X. "Ingrid, tell me about your neighbors' lives. Did they lose their jobs like you?"

Ingrid nodded. "Among the four on our street, the Jackson's are a very nice family with five children. They helped us so much during and after Rob's surgery and chemo. Mr. Jackson had a stroke and couldn't work the last two years. Thank God he's getting better and I believe starts back to work next month. He had very good health insurance and a good boss. Since his memory isn't the same, his boss is giving him another position he can manage. His wife is scared that the stress may cause her husband to have another stroke. If they are put out of their home, with five young children, I don't know what will happen to them." Ingrid paused, collected herself and continued. "We are so lucky to have you; you've become our angel. I pray that God will send them an angel to protect their health and their home, too."

"You said there are four homes on this street, not including yours. What about the other three homes?"

Rob took a tray of chocolate chip cookies from the oven. The fragrance of freshly baked cookies now filled the kitchen. He brought a plate of cookies to the table, gave Ingrid's shoulders a quick rub, then sat down next to her.

"Rob, these are delicious. They turned out great," Ingrid said.

"Honey, it's your touch that makes everything more delicious."

Jennifer asked again, a bit more firmly, "Please, tell me about the other three homes on your street."

Rob nodded. "Right… Mr. and Mrs. Johnson are like my own parents. Ingrid and I love them dearly. We were at their home once or twice a week having a drink and enjoying their lush garden. But since the foreclosure, they have isolated themselves. Often when I ring their doorbell to check on them, they don't answer or are very short with me."

Ingrid added, "They're retired. Very nice people. You've probably seen them walking their black Beagle, Snoopy. They didn't have children, so Snoopy is their baby. Anyways, they always wanted to go on a European cruise. Mr. Johnson's parents were from Poland and he wanted to connect with his roots before he leaves this world. So, he questioned a loan officer about getting a credit card with a two- to three-thousand-dollar limit for their cruise. He was encouraged to get a loan with a very low interest rate against their home. The mortgage payments were within their means. However, they didn't know that the interest rate they were given was a teaser rate. Not too long after, the rate went up, and their mortgage payment was triple the original amount.

"They became tempted to not only travel, but also to get a new car. Their car was old, and I had picked them up a few times from the mechanic's shop.

"Soon enough, they couldn't afford the higher mortgage payment and their home went into foreclosure. Mr. Johnson blames himself, the same as Rob. They feel they didn't protect their wives."

Ingrid went on to describe the lives of the other families on their street and in their neighborhood. It was heartbreaking to hear and speak about so much devastation and pain.

Rob poured freshly brewed coffee into Jennifer and Ingrid's cups, took a sip from his, and turned to Jennifer. "Jennifer, do you think we should come with you to the auction tomorrow?"

"No… I think it would be better not to," she answered.

"Why is that?" Ingrid asked, sounding impatient.

"Although we aren't related, the bank doesn't want the home to be sold to someone who's related to the homeowner."

"That doesn't make sense," Rob said.

"I think the bank doesn't want an owner to buy back their own foreclosed property and end up with the same house at a lower price than their existing loan with the bank."

The next day, Jennifer was at the auction for foreclosed homes in Erie. The place was crowded, full of investors, real estate agents, and homeowners.

In the crowd, she saw two of her high school classmates, John and Andy. She waved, and then walked toward them.

"Wow, Jennifer. What are you doing here?" Andy said.

"I'm here to bid on some of the houses."

"Why here? You left for college and never came back."

"I'm here now. Why are you here, Andy?"

"I'm a contractor. I buy fixer-uppers, fix them and sell them."

"How about you, John?"

John said, "I'm a realtor. I assist Andy in purchasing the properties, then help sell them after he remodels. Most of these houses need a lot of work. Maybe after you purchase, Andy can fix the properties up for you and I can sell them at a high price."

"Andy, which areas are you focused on buying?"

"Erie. We're still living there, unlike you, deserting your hometown." Jennifer couldn't tell if he was joking.

She said, "I'm so glad our paths crossed today. Are you guys married? Any children?"

Andy said, "I'm married. Three kids, a boy and two girls."

"How about you, John?"

He answered, "I was married. Divorced. No one in my life right now."

"How about children?" she asked.

"I have a boy who lives in Washington D.C. Tell us about yourself."

"I have a daughter who lives in New York."

Andy asked, "Are you married?"

"I was, to my daughter's father, but we divorced many moons ago."

John looked Jennifer up and down. "Are you coming back to Erie for good?"

"My plans aren't clear yet."

Andy, looking anxious, said, "I hope we aren't going to bid against each other."

Jennifer smiled. "Let's see how it plays out. Hopefully, we won't."

The three of them registered, received their bidding numbers, and walked to the room where the auction was being held. The auctioneer was already standing behind the podium, explaining how to bid. "In order to qualify for bidding, you must have a cashier's check for ten percent of the amount you are bidding."

All the seats were taken, except three in different rows.

At the end of the auction, Andy approached Jennifer looking very upset. "You ruined my day. Each time I bid on a property, you bid against me. Have I done something to you I'm not aware of?"

"Not at all. I have very good memories of you in high school."

"Then, why were you bidding against me?"

"I was sitting in the front row. You were in the row behind me. I couldn't see you. It seems both of us were interested in the same properties."

Jennifer's bid was the winning bid for Ingrid and Rob's home. Andy had the booklet in his hand, with the page showing their home. He came closer to Jennifer and showed the page to her, pointing out their home and said, "Jennifer, I'll give you five thousand dollars to transfer your rights to this house to me."

"Why?"

"Because this house is completely remodeled; it doesn't need much work. Don't be so greedy, you got ten houses. I'm only asking for this one, and I'm willing to pay you five thousand dollars for it."

"I am sorry. I can't do that."

"I don't understand. You said you weren't clear about moving to Erie permanently. Then you buy ten properties there, without seeming to care how much you were paying for them. It doesn't make sense."

"You're correct. Nothing makes sense in my life at this point."

He was getting angrier. "The only thing that makes sense is that you're a greedy woman. You were nice and considerate in high school. What happened to you?"

"Life circumstances change us. Did you end up buying anything?"

"I got one. Don't be like this. Just transfer that house to me."

"What's your plan if I did that?"

"I would sell it. The converted garage would make it an easy sale, even in this tough market."

"This means you don't have plans of moving in yourself, correct?"

"I wouldn't live in that part of town or in that small a house. I come to these auctions only to find good deals and make some profit."

John walked up at that moment and handed his card to Jennifer. "Use me when you decide to sell your properties. I'll charge you less commission, since we were high school buddies."

"Sorry, John, I won't be selling any of these properties."

"I also have a property management company. Many people who lost their homes are looking for rentals. You could get good, steady income from these properties."

"I won't be renting them, either."

Andy jerked his thumb at John, indicating he was ready to leave, and they walked away from Jennifer. Andy said, "The bitch messed up my day."

John said, "She's pretty. Do you think if I ask her on a date she'd accept?"

"Ask her on a date? Is it the bitch's looks or her money?" He tugged on his earlobe.

John brushed his palms together. "Stop it. There's something about her. In high school I had a crush on her, but I never had the courage to ask her out."

"Did she have a boyfriend in high school?"

"I don't think so… She was an honor student and an artist. I saw some of the portraits she painted. They were beautiful. Maybe she had a boyfriend, I don't remember. I think I am going to ask her out."

"Do you know where she lived?" He clenched his fists.

"As far as I remember, she was very private – didn't have many friends, except one…that girl with the mesmerizing blue eyes and short blond hair."

"Come on, seems like in high school you had a crush on every girl."

"Not every girl. Just a few," he sighed.

"Every week you were in love with a different girl."

"What can I say, I love women," John said.

"No. You just love the attention you get at the beginning. When the attention stopped, you moved on to the next girl. I remember in high school girls were warning each other to stay away from you. You were known as the heartbreaker."

"The good old days."

"You need to stop the chase," Andy told him.

"I know. That's the reason I'm going to therapy. I really want to patch up my relationship with my ex-wife."

"Do you think she will forgive you for cheating on her?"

"I hope so." He rubbed his forehead.

Andy changed the subject. "I keep wondering what Jennifer is up to. And what she wants to do with ten pieces of property in Erie."

"Maybe she wants to rent them out."

"I don't think so. She said she won't be renting them. And some of the properties she bought didn't make sense for income property."

"Maybe she wants to be your competition. Do the same thing you do: buy, fix, and sell."

When they got to the parking lot, Andy took his cell phone out and started a search on the internet.

"What was Jennifer's last name in high school?"

John furrowed his brows, then said, "I don't remember. She may have her husband's last name now."

"Is she still married? I thought she said she was divorced."

"I meant ex-husband."

"She said she was living in San Francisco. Come on, what was her last name?"

"It starts with an A. No, M. Maybe...W?" John shrugged.

"So much help." Andy shook his head, irritated.

"Try Johnson."

"No."

"How about Anderson?"

"No. It's not Anderson."

"Okay, I think I remember. Try Thompson."

Andy, in a surprised voice, said, "Wow! The bitch is super rich. Look, look... there are all these articles about her."

John glanced at the phone's tiny screen. "It's so strange. What's she doing in Erie? Why is she buying all these properties?"

"Look at this magazine. She's on the cover."

John moved closer for a better look. "Mama Mia, she's pretty. She was our classmate. Why didn't we know anything about her? Or how she became so rich?"

"If I knew this about her, maybe I would have been nicer to her. Learn about how she became so successful."

ॐ ॐ

Jennifer couldn't wait to give the good news to Ingrid and Rob. She dialed their number.

"Jennifer...is that you?" she heard Ingrid say.

"Yes. We got the house!"

Ingrid shouted, "We got the house! We got the house!" Jennifer could hear Rob in the background clapping his hands. Then he was at the phone, obviously with his arms around Ingrid, as they chorused, "Thank you, Jennifer!"

Rob laughed, then asked, "Can they change their minds if someone else offers more?"

"No! Nothing can be changed. The house is yours."

Rob couldn't believe it. "Life is so unpredictable. You saved us. You are our God-sent angel."

Jennifer allowed herself a brief laugh, then said, "Ingrid, I have a request."

"Anything you want. I am at your service."

"Please have a gathering at your home and ask the other neighbors whose homes were in foreclosure to come in three hours. I will be driving back from Pittsburg and it will take me that long to get there, depending on the traffic."

"Are you sure you want to see all of them?"

"Yes, please make sure they come. Let them know I was at the auction and I have some information about their homes."

"I feel so bad for them. While I am happy beyond words that you saved our home."

"Pizza on me. Order enough pizza for everyone so they can have something to munch on while we are there."

"Okay, Jennifer. As soon as I hang up, we'll go invite them all over. I think I can convince all of them to come, except maybe Mr. and Mrs. Johnson."

"Why is that?"

"Because they feel responsible for the foreclosures in the neighborhood."

"Why do they feel responsible for the others' foreclosures?"

"Because after they took out their loan, they bragged about the trip they took, which enticed other neighbors to refinance their homes, using the same loan officer as the Johnsons. So now they feel guilty, and some of the neighbors blame them for their misfortune."

Jennifer said, "Please, make sure they come as well."

"Okay, we'll do our best."

Jennifer hung up and began her drive from Pittsburg to Erie. She was excited and feeling alive. She hadn't had this kind of feeling in a long time. The anticipation of seeing Ingrid and Rob and their joy was heartwarming for her.

From the time she broke up with Babak, Jennifer's focus had been on the accumulation of wealth. She had changed her degree from art to business, then worked day and night until she opened her own company. She bought her first home, and then bought bigger and bigger homes. She was buying investment properties, investing in the stock market, and even playing the stock market in her spare time.

It seemed no matter how much she had; it was never enough. Her main intention was to make money, and to make sure money wasn't the reason her daughter would lose the love of her life. Life passed by without her noticing that she was in it.

Even when her offer was accepted among multiple offers to buy a big shopping center in San Francisco, it didn't give her joy. It just needed to be done. There was a hole in her heart that she was trying to fill with money, and no matter how much money she made, she couldn't fill that hole.

She was also blind to other people's needs. At work, she demanded performance; never seeing the pain or the struggles some of her employees faced daily. She never offered generous bonuses during Christmas holidays or to help them with unexpected expenses.

Even though she bought beautiful homes for her parents and her sister in an upscale neighborhood in Philadelphia, she didn't feel emotionally connected to that act or to them. She never went to visit and often didn't return their calls. Emotional connections were a burden for her.

She had sleepwalked through those years and her portfolio no longer had any meaning to her. All the dreams she worked so hard for had been shattered.

Her thoughts traveled far away, remembering a discussion with her daughter.

හ හ

"Anita, you're at Elizabeth's home all the time. Why don't you ask Isabella to come here once in a while?"

"Mom, you're never home. Even when you are home, you're always on the phone or on the computer."

Jennifer said, "You don't need me. You two can play together."

"I wish you were more like Elizabeth."

"Why is that?"

Anita explained, "She's always home when we arrive after school. Elizabeth plays with us or has an activity ready for Isabella and me to do. We paint together, and she is always very curious about our day at school."

"I bought you all those painting materials. You two can paint here."

"But you're not home. Elizabeth is fun, not serious like you."

"What do you mean?"

"Mom look at your home. This huge place with all white furniture. Full of expensive art pieces. It doesn't look or feel lived in. At Elizabeth's house, everything is lived in. The art pieces in her home are her art and Isabella's art. Even some of mine. Where in your home have you hung any of my art? None in the living room, none in the dining room, or family room. I have my art hanging in my room only."

"You can hang your art anywhere you want. I didn't know that it was important to you."

"When I say you don't see me and you are always in your head, this is one example of it."

"You know how much I love you. And my hard work is for your future."

"My future doesn't just need money. I can make it myself. What I need is love and connection. We never eat dinner together. When I go to my dad's house, my dad and his partner cook together, and I help out in the kitchen. They make cooking a fun adventure. Then we eat together and talk about our day. I feel they see me from the kind of questions they ask me. And they are all ears when I speak."

Jennifer tried to see things from her point of view. "If having dinner is so important to you, from now on we will plan to eat together."

"It's not just about eating together. Even when we traveled to places together like Australia or Europe, you were not emotionally with me. Financially, you were doing everything to make me happy. But I never saw your excitement, your laughter, or your own joy."

"My excitement was and is to see you happy. To see you excited."

"Life is not all about me. How about your own joy? Your own happiness, apart from mine?"

"This is such a deep discussion for a young daughter of mine. How about we continue another time?"

❧ ❧

Jennifer's phone was ringing, interrupting her deep thoughts. She used the speaker to answer. It was Ingrid. "Ingrid, what's going on?"

"I am here at Mr. and Mrs. Johnson's house. They don't want to come to our home. I told them you have some news about their home. However, they don't want to face the other neighbors. I thought you might be able to convince them to come."

"Let me talk to them."

Jennifer could hear Ingrid say, "Her name is Jennifer. She is the God-sent angel for us. I told you, she bought our home at the auction, and will allow us to stay at our home. She has news about your home. Talk to her."

"Hello?" Jennifer said.

"This is Emily Johnson."

"Mrs. Johnson. I am Jennifer Thompson. I am on my way back from the real estate auction that was held in Pittsburg. I truly want you to come to Ingrid and Rob's home. I am looking forward to meeting you and Mr. Johnson. I have some news about your home, which I want to give to you in person."

"Jennifer, thank you for the invitation. However, we can't face our neighbors. We don't go anywhere."

"It's just Ingrid and Rob's home."

"I understand. But our neighbors will be there, too. Since our homes went to foreclosure, we haven't been out very much. We can't face our neighbors' hardships. We are the reason their homes are in foreclosure."

"I promise you, when you show up at Ingrid and Rob's home, with the information I have, it will make you and your neighbors happy."

"Nothing can make us happy."

No matter how much Jennifer tried to convince them to come, they refused. After Jennifer and Mrs. Johnson ended their conversation, Jennifer's thoughts settled on her daughter again.

80 80

"But why New York? UC Berkeley or Stanford are much better schools."

"I want to get away and experience new things in my life."

"Why New York?"

Anita told her, "I don't want your kind of life for myself."

"I don't understand. What do you mean?"

Anita took too long to answer her mother's question. "Your life is too flashy for me."

Jennifer raised her eyebrows. "When you are financially successful, you can buy things without worrying about the price."

Anita softened her voice. "At the price of having no intimate connection. How often do you have guests at your home? How about a life partner?"

"What are these questions?" She rolled her eyes.

"Mom, you are detached from feeling. You do all the right things. However, emotionally, you're detached."

Jennifer dragged her hand through her hair repeatedly. "What do you mean emotionally detached? I would die for you."

"I know you love me. And you would do anything to make me happy."

"Then what is the problem?" Her eyes grew wet and her vision became blurry.

"Mom, I love you. And would love to see you happy. You are not happy."

"Happiness has different meanings for different people. Maybe my happiness is to make sure you are not deprived of anything in your life."

Anita's voice rose. "Again, you are talking about me not being *financially* deprived."

Jennifer cleared her throat and tried to find the right thing to say. "What is wrong with being financially strong?"

"Being financially strong is great. As long as nothing else is being sacrificed."

Jennifer was still confused. "Then what is the issue here?"

"Mom, it is hard for me to watch you, knowing you are not happy."

"Stay in the Bay Area and I will be happy."

"Mom, I told you, I have decided I'm going to New York. Don't get me wrong. I am very proud of you as a single mom, raising me without any help, not even from my father. You have become so successful."

"Why do you think I am not happy? The joy of having you in my life is all the happiness I need."

"Mom, you need other sources of joy and laughter in your life. You keep everyone at arm's length. You meet your friends at a restaurant only for lunch or dinner. Never at home to be relaxed with them. Elizabeth is the only one I've seen at our home. Then you have those big catered parties for your employees and friends once or twice a year. To me, it seems you are afraid of emotionally connecting to anyone."

Jennifer tried to explain. "People are different, and they desire different types of joy in their lives. Maybe what makes me happy is not the same thing as what makes Elizabeth happy."

"I agree. The reason I am bringing this up is because I don't see passion or joy in your work either. It seems you have a goal to be rich and to obtain a certain amount of wealth. However, work is a chore for you, not a joy."

"Running a company is not easy. Sometimes it feels like a chore."

೮ ೮

A car in front of Jennifer stopped suddenly in order to avoid hitting a deer on the road. Jennifer also hit the brakes and was lucky enough that the cars behind her were not close enough to rear-end her.

Her train of thought shifted with the sudden jolt of reacting quickly and she started thinking about the gathering at Ingrid and Rob's home. She couldn't wait to get there. This was a different feeling of joy and happiness. It had been such a long time since she had felt it.

She muttered to herself, "I was so wrapped up with the loss of Babak that I failed to notice other people's pain or struggle, or how much I could be helping someone else."

Her mind went to Elizabeth and the discussion she had with her.

ꙮ ꙮ

"Jennifer, why do you stay at home alone on Christmas Day? Come with us."

"No, I prefer to stay home."

"There is so much joy in giving food to hungry people. There are so many ways you can help at the soup kitchen."

"I can help out with money."

"It's not the same. They need the money, but on Christmas Day, don't eat at home alone. Anita's at her dad's; come with us. I'm sure when you see the smiles on their faces and the way they enjoy the food, like it's their first and last meal of their lives, it will put a smile on your face and fill your heart with joy," Elizabeth said.

"It's just not me. I can't imagine myself working in the soup kitchen."

"You are wrong, my dear friend. You need it more than any of us."

"Thank you, Dr. Elizabeth, for prescribing soup kitchen to fix my broken heart."

"You don't want to fix it, because you are not taking a chance with another man."

"If I say yes to taking a chance with another man, would you drop the subject?"

"Yes, my lips are zipped."

ॐ ॐ

As she drove along, Jennifer's thoughts jumped around to different times in her life – like the time she found out she was pregnant.

ॐ ॐ

"Jennifer, are you throwing up again?" Elizabeth asked.

"I think I have the stomach flu."

"Do you have a fever?"

"No. It's the smell of your Chinese food."

"It has been more than a week that you've been feeling like this. You need to be checked by a doctor," Elizabeth told her.

"Maybe in a few days. I'll get better."

"I'm worried about you. Since Babak left for Paris you have just been in your bed. It's like you've given up living. You're not going to school. You're not eating. Enough is enough. Get out of bed. You haven't even taken a shower for the last few days."

"I will. I will."

"You say you will, but you don't."

"Sorry. I'm about to throw up." Jennifer grabbed the wastebasket near her bed and leaned over it.

"I can't watch you waste your life like this." Elizabeth picked up Jennifer's raincoat, held it in front of her face, and said, "Let's go."

"Where?"

"To see a doctor." Elizabeth took Jennifer's hand and pulled her out of bed.

"Leave me alone."

"I can't. Let's go."

Jennifer looked very weak, with puffy eyes and uncombed, dirty hair. Elizabeth continued to give orders. "Put on your raincoat. Let's go."

At this point, Jennifer didn't have the energy to argue and they left to see a doctor.

After seeing the doctor, they had to sit in the waiting room until the doctor received the test results. The receptionist had a very outgoing personality and liked to talk. As soon as Jennifer and Elizabeth sat down, she said, "What's troubling our patient?"

Jennifer didn't respond, so Elizabeth said, "She can't eat anything and has constant nausea. The smell of food bothers her, even the smell from the restaurant across the street. We need to find out what's going on."

Elizabeth took Jennifer's hand and said, "I told you not to break up with Babak. Your heartbreak caused all this."

Jennifer looked miserable. About this time, the chatty receptionist left her desk and brought a box of crackers to Elizabeth.

"I bet she's pregnant. As you can see, I am pregnant, too. During the first few months of my pregnancy, I often threw up and the smell of some foods was just terrible. These crackers have been a lifesaver for me."

Elizabeth took the crackers, handed one to Jennifer, and in a commanding voice said, "Eat."

Jennifer nibbled at a cracker, and to Elizabeth's surprise, she seemed to enjoy it. And she didn't even show any adverse reaction. Elizabeth handed her one after another.

The receptionist was watching them and said, "Didn't I tell you she's pregnant? I can bet when the doctor gets the results that will be the diagnosis. One day she is going to wake up and will want to eat like a horse. Now that I'm this far along in my pregnancy, I want to eat non-stop."

Elizabeth responded, "I hope it is just the stomach flu, not a pregnancy or serious illness."

A little later, the nurse came to the waiting room and asked Jennifer to follow her. Both girls got up and followed the nurse to the doctor, who looked at Jennifer and said, "The good news is that you are healthy and nothing is wrong with you—"

Before the doctor finished his sentence, Elizabeth jumped in. "She cannot eat. She throws up continuously."

The doctor smiled, then continued. "Congratulations. Jennifer, you are pregnant. All these symptoms are due to your pregnancy. The body's hormones change and different women react differently."

The room had started to spin like they were on a merry-go-round. The doctor repeated his diagnosis. "You're pregnant. You are experiencing the symptoms of pregnancy."

ॐ ॐ

Jennifer saw a supermarket along the way and stopped to buy a case of champagne, a few cases of soda, and three cakes: chocolate, strawberry cheesecake, and a tiramisu.

At the cashier, she noticed the person ahead of her didn't have enough money to pay for all his grocery items. He was handing items back to the cashier to remove from his purchase, asking the cashier how much the bill would be after those items were taken off. He was struggling to decide which items to give to the cashier, since it seemed that he really needed everything in his cart.

Jennifer stepped forward, telling the cashier, "Here's my credit card. Please charge his groceries to it, including what he was going to leave behind."

As the gentleman pushed his cart full of groceries to the exit door, he stopped and turned back to look at Jennifer. The tears running down his face told more than any spoken words about how thankful he was for Jennifer's generous gesture.

Jennifer put her purchases in the trunk and headed on to Ingrid and Rob's home with memories of her pregnancy still on her mind.

৪৩ ৪৩

"Elizabeth, how am I going to take care of a child with no money and no husband? What kind of future is that for a child?"

"Jennifer, you need to take care of *you*. Maybe you need to have an abortion."

"No way. Babak is the father."

"You're not thinking straight. At least consider putting the child up for adoption."

"No way. I want to hold my baby in my arms. This baby is Babak's child, too."

Elizabeth said, "Do you want to keep the baby because you are hoping the baby will gain the approval of Babak's family?"

"No. I know they will never approve of us being together. I want the baby because Babak is the father."

"What about your life?"

"My life from now on is about my child. This child deserves to have everything, not to be deprived like I was."

"How are you going to give your baby everything with the situation you're in? Sometimes giving everything to a child is finding them a good home, and maybe the adoption could give your child the home she or he deserves."

"I can't even think about adoption. This baby is Babak's baby, too. I will take care of my child. I will find a way to provide for the baby. And I won't allow anything or anyone to interfere with my child's happiness."

"How are you going to explain your pregnancy to your parents?" Elizabeth asked.

"I am worried about how it will hurt my mother, especially. My mother was worried that if I went to Paris I might stop going to school and end up having kids and become a homemaker like her. Well, I am not in Paris, I'm not in school, and I am pregnant."

ॐ ॐ

Finally, Jennifer arrived at Ingrid and Rob's home. She parked her car in the driveway and rang the doorbell. It was three o'clock in the afternoon. A sunny day. Most everyone was gathered in the kitchen, with some in the backyard.

Ingrid opened the door, put her arms around Jennifer, and hugged her. "Thank you. Thank you. Thank you!"

Jennifer told her, "I bought some food for today. Let's go to the car and bring it in."

"Everyone is waiting for you. They are anxious. What kind of news do you have for them?"

"Very, very good news."

Jennifer and Ingrid came back into the house with bags of groceries. Rob spotted them and hurried to pull the cases of drinks from the car and take them to the kitchen.

As soon as Jennifer entered, all eyes were immediately on her. Rob set his burden aside and made introductions to those gathered. "Everyone, this is Jennifer Thompson."

Jennifer took a step forward, shaking each neighbor's hand as they introduced themselves. There were eight couples: The Smiths, the Browns, the Millers, the Richardsons, the Bennetts, the Jacksons, the Wilsons, and the Williams'.

When Jennifer shook Mrs. Richardson's hand, the woman kept hold of Jennifer's hand and asked, "Don't you remember me? We went to the same elementary school."

"You look familiar. Were we classmates?"

"Yes. I'm Olivia."

As soon as she said her name, Jennifer's mind spun away. She was remembering fourth-grade recess when Olivia was chanting, 'Jennifer's father is a garbage man. Jennifer's father is our garbage man.' And all the other kids were giggling. Ingrid touched Jennifer on the shoulder and said, "I went to the same elementary school. I am surprised I never noticed you two there."

Olivia responded, "It was and still is a big elementary school. And we were not in the same class." She turned to Jennifer, "How long are you staying in town?"

"My plans are not clear yet."

Rob opened the champagne bottles and handed each neighbor a glass, while they waited for the pizza to arrive.

Jennifer took her glass and said, "Let's drink to our health. And the news that none of you have to move from your homes."

Suddenly the room was filled with many loudly voiced questions. Mrs. Brown started out saying, "Jennifer, today was the auction. Who owns our home now?"

"I bought your home."

"Why?"

"To help you out."

"How will you help us out?"

Mr. Brown then jumped into the conversation. "Let's hear Jennifer out. She may have some suggestions for us. Even a few more months living at our homes would give us a huge break."

Jennifer smiled. "I was in Pittsburg today at the auction where all of your homes were up for sale. There were many bidders; however, I won the bids on your homes. I got all ten homes, including Mr. and Mrs. Johnson's."

Mrs. Wilson, looking very upset, said, "What's your plan now? You buy ten pieces of property at once while we couldn't even keep up with one. This is the way the rich become richer, and the poor become poorer. It's not fair."

Rob stepped in. "Mrs. Wilson, Jennifer is here to help us. It is not her fault we are in this situation. Jennifer, please continue."

But Mrs. Wilson didn't stop, continuing on before Jennifer could say a word. "It is hard for rich people to understand our lives. One month ago, we were evicted from our home. Most of our belongings are still in the house. And we are living with two young kids in Mr. and Mrs. Smith's garage. Their home was foreclosed on as well, and when they're evicted we will have to sleep on the street until we can find jobs."

Mrs. Wilson continued, "We're willing to work. We're hard workers, and we don't mind any kind of job. With all these layoffs, we have even lost hope for living. Who can blame me if I'm angry and if I blame greedy rich people?"

Ingrid took Mrs. Wilson's hand and said, "Let's go to the yard and get some fresh air." As they walked out of the kitchen, Jennifer continued.

"I am so sorry for the circumstances you are in. Mrs. Wilson is correct. The unfairness exists. Especially at a time like this. I noticed how investors are capitalizing on homeowners' misfortunes. I bid on your homes because I want to help you get your homes back, so you don't have to move. And if you've already been evicted, to allow you to move back."

Questions were fired at her one after another, asking how they would be able to buy back their homes. Mrs. Brown asked what they all were thinking, "How are we getting our homes back when we don't have a penny to spare?"

"My attorney will be in touch with each of you about all the necessary steps. You will need to fill out a loan application. Then we will deed the property back to you. We will become your lender, and your loan amount will be what we paid at the auction for each house. Any payment you make will go toward your principal, reducing your loan amount."

"Are you saying you won't charge us interest?"

"I will charge the same amount I would be receiving if my money were in a savings account. Which, in this market, is less than one percent," Jennifer explained.

Olivia said, "Jennifer, my husband and I are out of work. We don't have money to pay the mortgage. Does this mean we can't get our home back?"

"We will work with you until you find a job. The economy won't be like this forever, and in a few years the job market will improve and property values will go up. The most important part is that you don't lose your home. Life has its own ups and downs. Be positive and hopeful until a job comes your way."

Suddenly, the atmosphere in the room changed. Everyone surrounded Jennifer, some with tears in their eyes, thanking her. Jennifer quickly handed out slips from the auction that showed the bids for their properties so they could see that this was all real.

Mr. Wilson said, "Angels come in different shapes and forms. You are truly our angel. We never imagined our lives ending up like this. Practically homeless or ending up on the street. You saved us. You saved us!"

Mrs. Wilson, who had been in the backyard, came to Jennifer, tears in her eyes, and said, "We never will forget your generosity. You saved us. You saved us from being homeless. You saved our two girls."

"Mrs. Wilson, I am so happy to be a small help. All of us sometimes need a helping hand to move forward in life. I grew up here. My father was a garbage collector in this neighborhood. I witnessed the sacrifice my parents endured when I was growing up in this home."

Jennifer realized she was talking about her father being a garbage man without any shame. Not only did she not feel shame, she felt very proud of her dad for who he was.

Jennifer then waved a hand to quiet the room down. "We asked Mr. and Mrs. Johnson to join us; however, they refused. How about we take some food and all go to their home to give them the good news as well? They feel guilty about introducing their lender to you years back."

Mr. Bennett blurted out, "They should feel guilty. If they hadn't bragged about their loan, I wouldn't be in this situation. I was working and paying my mortgage. The lender suddenly raised the rate on the loan and my mortgage payment ballooned to three times the original."

"I understand you're upset. Are you upset with Mr. and Mrs. Johnson? Or are you upset with yourself?"

"Of course I'm upset with them."

"Did they ask you to refinance your home?" Jennifer asked him.

"What's the difference? Because they bragged, we ended up with a refinance."

Jennifer drew in a long breath. "Who filled out the loan application?"

"We did."

"Who signed the loan documents?"

Mr. Bennett threw his hands in the air. "We did."

"Did you read the loan documents?"

"No…we didn't… We went by what the Johnson's said."

Jennifer continued, "If you had read the loan documents, you would have seen that your rate was variable and would be increased after the initial period. You would not normally have signed for such a loan. In your situation, who should be blamed? Mr. Johnson? Or you?"

"I guess I could have ignored his bragging."

"And…"

"Read the loan documents and realized the rate would go up. I needed to listen to my gut feeling and not sign the documents."

"How would you feel now if all of us go to Mr. and Mrs. Johnson's home?"

"I understand that we were responsible…not Mr. Johnson."

"Then let's go to Mr. and Mrs. Johnson's."

They all walked down the street to Mr. and Mrs. Johnson's home with the cake, champagne, and pizza and knocked on the door. Mrs. Johnson opened the door.

Jennifer smiled, champagne in hand. "Mrs. Johnson, we spoke earlier about you and Mr. Johnson coming to Ingrid and Rob's house. Since you couldn't come, we came to you."

Mrs. Johnson's eyes went wide with surprise. Mr. Johnson came to the door and immediately invited everyone inside.

When they entered the house, Jennifer noticed all the windows were covered with thick curtains and their home looked much bigger than Ingrid and Rob's. The house was also built on a very large lot with a big backyard.

Rob took the initiative, asking, "May I open the curtains?"

Mr. Johnson nodded, and Rob pulled the curtains open. From the large living room, they could see into the backyard, which was overgrown with vegetation and dead trees, as well as many dried out potted plants.

As soon as Ingrid saw the backyard she said, "What happened to your backyard? I loved it when I visited. It was always in full bloom from spring to fall with so many beautiful flowers."

Mr. Johnson replied, "This recession, followed with the foreclosure of our home, took the life out of us. I prayed that we would die before we were evicted at our age—"

Mrs. Johnson interrupted. "What is the occasion for all of you being here?"

Rob said, "We are here to share our good news with you."

"What kind of news is good at a time like this?"

At this point, Mr. Bennett took Mr. Johnson's hand and said, "Please forgive me. I have been blaming you for our situation. You didn't do anything wrong and have been a good neighbor. You just shared your information with us. What we decided to do with the information was our own responsibility."

"I can't forgive myself. I have been blaming myself and wishing I never took the trip or got the loan," Mr. Johnson explained.

"What took place is in the past. We are here to show you that we are not upset with you. Also, Jennifer Thompson has some very good news for you."

"I'm confused. What are you talking about?"

Jennifer told Mr. and Mrs. Johnson about buying their home and that she planned to transfer the deed to them. Everyone shared in the Johnsons' joy.

Shortly, Ingrid, Rob, and Jennifer said goodbye to everyone and walked back to Ingrid and Rob's home. Ingrid took Jennifer's hand, saying, "What a day. You made so many neighbors of mine filled with joy."

Jennifer smiled and softly replied, "The joy was all mine."

"I hope you are feeling good about yourself for being such a kind and generous person."

The kind of feelings Jennifer was experiencing were unfamiliar to her. For the first time in twenty-five years, she felt grateful for what she had and that she had enough wealth to help others, rather than just add to her own wealth. Her mind was occupied with thinking about how she could help more people.

When they reached the house, they sat around the kitchen table. Rob said, "I drank too much. Do you mind if I make a pot of coffee?"

Jennifer replied, "I think I drank beyond my limit as well. It must be the champagne, the way I feel."

Ingrid became curious and said, "How are you feeling? I hope you're okay."

"I am feeling above the clouds, and so joyous. These feelings are so unfamiliar to me. That's the reason I think it's the effect of too much champagne."

Ingrid said, "Not a chance. The way you feel is because so many people will sleep peacefully tonight, saved from the worry of being homeless. And it's all thanks to you."

"There's so much going on in my life, it doesn't allow room for joy or happiness."

"How many people do you think are sending you prayers and good wishes? Rob and I are two of them. All of your problems will be solved, the same as you brought a solution to our nightmares."

"I am thinking and thinking about how I can help the other homeowners before their homes go into foreclosure."

"Jennifer, you have done enough for one day. Stay with the good feelings you have."

"I have some ideas, and maybe jobs for both of you."

"Jennifer, as your friend, I want you to go back to San Francisco to face whatever is so painful for you. Talk to your daughter."

"I can't... I'm not ready yet."

When the night ended, Jennifer went upstairs and opened the bedroom door. She sat on the bed, her hands on top of each other, covering her heart. She was smiling, and it seemed she was trying to hold onto her joyous feeling. She whispered, "Elizabeth was right."

She remembered when she was painting, how happy she was. When she finished a portrait, she was so joyful. It was like she was the luckiest person in the world. She felt so proud of herself, and her life. Her passion for life, her kindness, and her generosity were known by her friends, and she was loved by all her classmates.

Elizabeth's voice was ringing in her ears...

⁎ ⁎

"Jennifer, you didn't go to class again. You're missing so many classes."

Jennifer said, "I'm thinking about changing my major."

"What are you talking about?"

"I am thinking about changing it to business…"

"Why?"

"An art major doesn't make much money, even if we're lucky enough to find a job as a teacher."

"But being a teacher was your dream," Elizabeth said.

"Not anymore."

"Why?"

"Because I'm pregnant."

"All the more reason for you to finish your degree."

"I will be responsible for my child's future. And I want my child to have money. Lots of money."

"What does money have to do with changing your major? Being a teacher will give us a decent salary to live on."

"That's not enough for me."

"What happened to you? As long as I can remember, you were talking about teaching art to children. You were the one lecturing me about how art connects us to our souls."

"I don't want my child to experience what I experienced."

Elizabeth knew what she was really thinking. "I know giving up Babak has been very hard on you."

"He has no way to contact me. He forgot to take his address book; he left it here. And I don't know where in Paris he lives. I wish there was a way to know how he is doing. I miss him so much."

"Let's focus on your classes."

"I'm serious. I'll change my major to business."

"What will a business degree give you that an art degree can't?"

"I told you. Money. I want to be wealthy. So rich that my wealth is so much more than the parents of any potential person my child wants to marry in the future."

"My, my… What's going on? Just because you're pregnant you're changing your life path because of your child's future marriage? Your child may fall in love with a poor person. Even on a teacher's salary, you would have more money than them."

"What would happen if my child falls in love with someone from a rich family?"

"Your child will figure it out. All rich families are not like Babak's. Being a teacher may not mean lots of money, but it's a respected job."

"My mind is made up."

"You're making a big mistake. The biggest mistake of your life. You love drawing and painting. Your paintings are so advanced. Several times I have heard the teachers talking about your artwork. You might even sell your paintings in galleries and become rich and famous that way."

"It's a long shot to think I'll sell my art in galleries."

Elizabeth said in a serious voice, "You lost your spirit the night you left the Persian New Year party at Babak's parents' home."

"If my parents had money, Babak and I would be together now."

"Tell me, how did you feel when you left the party?"

"I felt so small. And so angry at my father for having a job as a garbage man. I was mad at my parents for running away together and creating a life like that for us."

"What else?"

"I felt shame for not having money and not being able to stand up to Babak's family. It was so awful when I left the party. I could hear them, the way they were talking about me. I wanted to die in that moment."

"Your spirit died. You've changed. You're not the same Jennifer I knew for so many years."

"What do you mean?"

"The Jennifer I knew would never give up art for money. And not return her parents' calls."

"I told you, I am upset with them."

"Upset with them because they didn't have enough money for Babak's parents to approve of you? If you are not with Babak, it's not your parents' fault. It was your decision."

"How can you say it was my decision? You know I didn't have a choice."

"You had the choice to go to Paris with him. Rehashing your mother's life stopped you," she was starting to get angry.

"I couldn't stand him feeling guilty and sad, the same as my mother."

"How many times have I told you that no two experiences are the same? If I were you, I would have gone to Paris. There was a chance he could convince his uncle and cousin not to say anything. And the possibility for his parents to agree for the two of you to be together. Or if the uncle and cousin report back to the parents about you, and the parents didn't come around and accept you, at least you would have a free trip to Paris!"

"I knew his parents wouldn't change their minds. You don't know the Persian culture."

"True. I'm not familiar with Persian culture. But I know the love between a mother and her child. And there was a good chance they would come around and accept you."

"His mother would rather die before seeing me with Babak."

Elizabeth tried to reason with her. "Let me ask you this… Let's pretend that Babak's parents come around and accept you two being together. What would your decision be then? To run to Babak? Or to stay away?"

"I would run to Babak." She hesitated, "No, I can't."

"Why can't you?"

"I can't stand the way they looked at me before I left the party. Their eyes. All of them, his mother's and the guests'. Those eyes are haunting me. They made me feel ashamed of myself and my family. I became small, very small. The only way I know how to be me again is by becoming rich."

"Hypothetically speaking, if Babak's parents approve of you two being together, you would still stay away from Babak? Is that what you're saying?"

"I don't know. Most likely, yes, I would stay away until I was rich. That's the reason I need to change my major to business. I need to be rich."

"My friend, you are making the biggest mistake of your life. I repeat that. The *biggest* mistake of your life. You won't feel okay. You won't feel happy. Even if you become the richest woman in America."

"I've made my decision."

❧ ❧

Jennifer's thoughts were interrupted by footsteps in the hallway. Ingrid and Rob were going to their bedroom. Her train of thought switched, and she started thinking about creating a company to help people who are going through hardships and have fallen behind on their mortgage payments.

She opened her laptop and began researching how to provide such help and create jobs as well. The whole night she was awake, doing her research and making notes. Finally, at five o'clock in the morning, she went to sleep, her laptop and note-book next to her pillow.

Ingrid and Rob were in the kitchen the next morning. The coffee was ready, and Rob was about to make an omelet, but he was waiting for Jennifer to come down. They waited for a while. It wasn't like her to wake up so late. Finally, Ingrid went upstairs and knocked on the bedroom door. Jennifer didn't answer, so Ingrid opened the door, and saw that Jennifer was in a deep sleep. She went next to the bed and very gently said, "Jennifer, are you okay?"

Jennifer opened her eyes. "What time is it?"

"Ten a.m."

"Oh my. I'm getting up."

Rob started to make the omelets and they sat in their usual spots at the table. Jennifer took a deep swallow from her cup of coffee. She couldn't wait to share her plans she worked on last night.

Ingrid scooped up a bite of omelet. "Jennifer, let's do something today to celebrate."

Jennifer gave Ingrid a bright smile. "I have decided to open a company here."

"What do you mean?"

"I want to put both of you to work."

"Jennifer, I told you yesterday. You have unfinished business in San Francisco. You need to go back and talk to your daughter. After that, if you decide to come back, we will welcome you."

Rob interrupted. "Let's hear what kind of company she wants to open."

Jennifer went on, "It will be a financial company…similar to a mortgage brokerage."

"How would that work?"

"First, we have to establish a corporation. My attorney will work on that. We would need a physical address. For now, we can use this address and use the garage until we move to a permanent address.

"We'll concentrate on houses that are behind on their mortgage payments in the Erie area and surrounding cities, all the way to Pittsburg. Rob would go to the city halls of each city to check notices of default filed on a property. The record of it would include the property address, the owner's name, and the lender information.

"When Rob has a list, you two would contact the owners. If they're still working, and their mortgage rate is up to where they can't pay their mortgage, we'll create a contract with them, without any upfront charge, and negotiate on their behalf with the lenders to reduce their loan amount. This might also be done through extending the length of the loan, which would decrease their monthly payment or lower their interest rate. Or a combination of approaches.

"If we're successful with the banks, then we would take a percentage of the reduced loan amount, plus any upfront money we may pay, to bring their mortgage current."

Rob put plates in the sink, then returned to the table. "What happens if the lender doesn't want to cooperate to lower the loan amount or reduce the interest rate or extend the terms of the loan?"

"If we can't get any cooperation from the lender, then we'll provide the lender with comparable sales to show them the property value is much less than the loan amount against the property. And we'll try to pay off the loan at a reduced amount. If the bank agrees to this approach, then we'll become the lender."

Rob nodded thoughtfully. "If the bank doesn't cooperate, what happens to the homeowner and their loan?"

"We may not be able to help everyone. Even if we help ten to twenty percent of the ones we contact, we will have accomplished a lot and helped many people in need."

Leaning forward in his chair, Rob asked, "Will the homeowner be able to stay at their home?"

"It will be their choice. Whether to stay or find a tenant for the property."

Rob's eyes were wide as he listened to Jennifer. At the same time, he had so many questions. "How are we going to be paid?"

"You will contact our human resources department. They would establish a monthly salary for both of you. Then, by closing a property, whether we take a percentage or become the lender, you would receive a bonus."

Rob grinned and sat back. "Well, I'm on board. We haven't worked for so long; anything would be fine with us. We know how fair and helpful you are."

Ingrid had quietly listened to Rob and Jennifer's speculations, and now spoke up. "I'm worried about you going through so much expense... and if we couldn't help any of the homeowners, you would lose a lot of money."

Jennifer shook her head. "Any business has its risks. The focus needs to be on helping the homeowners rather than being afraid to take the risk."

Chapter 5

THE DARK...

Jennifer took a deep breath. She couldn't believe herself, the way she was talking. Her feeling of not having enough had vanished. Her focus and goals in life had changed one hundred-eighty degrees. She was still deeply hurt and confused about her future. But her focus on helping others was helping her survive during this tough period of her life.

Again, Ingrid pressed Jennifer. "You need to go back to San Francisco. The first thing you need to do now is deal with what was so troublesome for you that it brought you here."

"My mind is made up. I need to get this project off the ground."

Rob got up from his chair and said, "I have to leave you two ladies now and go to Mr. and Mrs. Johnson's home."

Ingrid asked, "What's the occasion?"

"Last night I suggested to some of the neighbors that we help with the clean out of Mr. and Mrs. Johnson's garden. So, five of us are going over there now to get dirty."

Ingrid smiled. "Oh, what a great idea! That backyard was like heaven. When I went there, I didn't want to leave because it was so peaceful and calming."

"And that's exactly why we want to help out and bring it to life again."

Jennifer asked, "Are you planting new trees to replace the dead ones?"

Rob said, "No. We're just clearing it out. I don't think Mr. and Mrs. Johnson have the means to buy trees."

"How about trees, flowers, and plants on me? Here's my credit card."

"Are you sure?" Rob hesitated to take the offered card.

"Yes, I am."

Rob headed for the living room and tossed his hat in the air. "I can't wait to see the garden back to its original glory." And then he was out the door.

Ingrid shook her head, smiling. "I think the Johnsons' garden represents our life. Hopefully, we are also going to be able to recover from the painful life we have been living and be renewed."

She turned to Jennifer, still wearing a peaceful smile. "Jennifer, I wish you had met with the therapist I recommended. I'm concerned that you're not dealing with your pain...well, that is to say that it seems you handle pain or fears by pretending they don't exist."

She took Jennifer's hand and held it, looking into her eyes. "I hope you know how much I care for you. You saved us from being homeless. From what you've told me, you were tormented by hurt feelings that began in the fourth grade, when your classmates made fun of your dad's job. You pretended you didn't see the kids that had said hurtful things. Then, you worked harder in school to become an honor student."

176

She gently shook Jennifer's hand to make sure she was still listening. "And when your brother died, you pretended it didn't happen, which kept you from mourning his death. Then, you started painting non-stop. When you and Babak broke up, you changed your life plan and your college focus to support becoming super rich, so you could shield your daughter from the shame and the hurt you felt the night of your engagement party."

Ingrid bowed her head for a moment, then went on, her voice soft and sad. "You missed the chance to have a loving and intimate relationship with Babak. You could have hired a private detective to find him in Paris, since you are clearly still in love with him. You could have done that ten or fifteen years ago. Or you could have allowed yourself to have an intimate, loving relationship with another man. And, no matter how rich you became, it was never enough because the wound from the night of that party remains untended in your psyche."

Ingrid paused, then took a deep breath. "I don't know the details of the phone call you had with your daughter, but I do know the shape you were in when you parked your car in front of our home. Please don't be upset with me and what I am about to say. I feel that you need to deal with your reaction to your daughter's call. You're falling back on old habits – pretending something didn't happen – while your mind focuses on a new driven idea: helping the world, so you can continue to postpone going back to San Francisco and dealing with the phone call that triggered all this."

Jennifer pulled her hand away and rolled her eyes. She got up, shaking her head. "You are mistaken. I am very much aware of the pain I'm carrying and what is ahead of me. However, my extreme pain evoked something in me, and I can now see other people's pain. And if I'm able to be a small help, I want to be that person. I want to give that help. You are correct that in the last twenty-five years my only focus has been to grow my wealth. I wasn't seeing anyone or anything beyond ways to make more money. And I never felt happy or joyous about what I gained. This is why the joy I felt from giving good news to the homeowners was so grand."

"That's what I am talking about. Listen for a moment please. You loved your brother. Your focus became painting. Any spare time was devoted to painting. Right?"

"Yes..."

"You loved Babak and sacrificed that intimate relationship. Your focus became the accumulation of wealth. You ran from the pain caused by your daughter's phone call. Now your focus is on helping the owners of your old house and other homeowners, who are strangers to you."

Jennifer didn't understand. "What are you saying?"

"I think that not dealing with your brother's death and the grief from that loss created a kind of pattern in your life. You discovered a way to insulate yourself when you experience something painful. You learned how to escape the grief process by putting all of your energy into something else... postponing dealing with the issue at hand... pretending it doesn't exist."

Ingrid paused and clasped her hands together, as in prayer. "Call your daughter. Tell her how you're feeling."

"Not yet. I am not ready." Jennifer stood by the table, tapping her fingertips against her lips.

Ingrid sat back, brows furrowed, then she smiled. "Let me ask you this. How many hours have you spent buying ten houses, getting ten cashier's checks, driving to Pittsburg, and thinking up and planning for a new company? I bet you have spent many, many hours. Now tell me, how many hours have you spent resolving the issue with your daughter?"

Jennifer slumped down onto the chair. "It's much easier to push it down and focus on something else."

"Pushing it down doesn't solve the problem."

"I know that."

"Let me dial your daughter's number…"

"No…not now."

Ingrid sighed, then reached for the stack of papers still on the kitchen table and held them up to Jennifer. "Then tell me about these poems. You were engaged?"

"Not now, another time," Jennifer said.

"You were married. I think I heard from my mother that you were married to David. Is that Anita's father?"

Jennifer looked beyond Ingrid and began speaking about David.

ಹಿ ಹಿ

"David, you know we can't get married. You're gay."

"And you're pregnant. How are you going to explain that to your family? The father of your child is in Paris, and you may never see him again," David said. "I am also from a very religious family. I can't tell my family about my desire to be with a man."

"So…what are you saying?"

"I'm saying, I will become the father to your child and both of us live as friends in marriage. I promise you; I will be the best father your child can have."

"Do you mean like two friends living in the same house?"

"Yes. Except that I will be a full participant as a father to your child. The baby will be ours – you the mother and me the father."

Jennifer was overwhelmed by the idea. "I have to think about this."

179

"There's nothing to think about. I just graduated and I have a job offer from a good firm. Your baby will have the father that he or she deserves."

"I'm not sure... I'm still grieving the loss of Babak."

"Our marriage will be a fake marriage, with the exception of fatherhood."

"What happens if Babak finds out he has a child and demands full custody or to be a part of the baby's life?"

"How could he find out?" David asked.

"I had to let Babak know about my pregnancy. Elizabeth and I went to Babak's home, but he was in Paris. The butler made us stand outside as he called for Babak's mother, who just yelled, 'What does she want this time? She has already done enough harm. She took my son away from me.' Then she came to the door and said, 'Why are you here? Babak is in Paris and already dating a nice girl, give it up.'

"I couldn't talk. Elizabeth stepped in and said, 'Babak needs to know that he's becoming a father. Jennifer is pregnant and the baby is Babak's.' Babak's mother called us crazy, said if I was pregnant, Babak was not the father, and called us whores. Elizabeth reminded her that she would be denying her grandchild, but Mrs. Frozan waved her hands in our faces, saying her son would marry a virgin, and that we needed to get out and never come back."

David groaned. "What a terrible woman! And such a harsh response to the news of becoming a grandmother. So...will you marry me?" He smiled broadly at her.

෫ ෫

Ingrid rose and put her arms around Jennifer's shoulders. "I am so sorry you had to endure such a cruel response. Do you care for a cup of tea?"

Jennifer nodded. They drank their tea in silence, until Ingrid asked, "Where is David now?"

"As we speak, David is in New York, meeting Anita's fiancé and his family."

"Are you still married to David?"

"No, I'm not."

"What happened?"

"He was gay. Four years into the marriage, he came out of the closet and that was the end of our marriage."

"I'm curious, was there any romance between the two of you?"

"If you mean sex – no. We never had sex. We were like two roommates pretending to be married."

Ingrid asked, "Why did you agree to that arrangement?"

"I don't know. I was heartbroken and pregnant. I didn't want to add to my mother's worry or pain by raising a child by myself. At least with David, my child could have a father."

"You are pretty and talented. Surely there were straight men who wanted to be with you. To love you and be a great father to Anita."

"I didn't want a romantic relationship. My heart belonged to Babak. The arrangement David and I had was perfect. My parents wouldn't worry about me. My child would have a father. And we were free to be ourselves, within the marriage."

"How is his relationship with Anita?"

"They are very close. David has been a great father to Anita."

"How about you two?"

"We're good friends." Jennifer took a deep breath and added, "I don't know how to tell my daughter."

"You haven't told Anita that Babak is her father?"

"No, David and I kept that secret. And David was and is such an amazing father."

"Why do you need to tell her now? Did Anita find out about David not being her father? Was the phone call from Anita about that?"

Jennifer didn't answer; so, Ingrid changed the subject. "Did you get married again?"

"No. I dated a few times, but by the second or third date I would stop going out. Once, I was engaged for three weeks."

"These poems must be about dating and your engagement. May I read them?"

"Yes."

Another Man

I had to say goodbye
To another man.

I looked at his eyes,
I didn't see your light.

I listened to his voice,
But it wasn't yours.

He didn't move like you,
He didn't sit or walk like you.

I couldn't find your smile,
Even when he was full of love.

I had to say goodbye
Because you are still in my heart.

Engaged

I became engaged today
To a very nice man.

I am sorry, my love,
I had to move on.

I think this way
My heart could find space
For someone else in my life.

I am looking at my engagement ring
With its big stone.
I see your face
Engraved in the diamond.

I pray to God
From now on
To remove you from my heart.

Break up

My fiancé broke up with me.
He gave his ring back
And said,
"You are still in love with him."

He was talking fast
And feeling sad
Because he couldn't find
Any room in my heart.

He was upset with you
Because he knew
You still own my heart
In spite of his love

I couldn't move on,
I can't come back to you.
Please tell me
What to do,
How not to suffer so much.

"It seems you are still in love with Babak…"

Jennifer nodded. "Yes. I am. That love never left me."

"Too bad. I suspect there are many nice men who would love to be with you. Such denial of true happiness…and to have just worked instead."

Jennifer said, "I don't know what's wrong with me. I just couldn't let him go. He's with me, in my heart, day and night. When I bought the red shoes for the party, I was in seventh heaven. Everything I wanted in my life I had. I was so happy and full of joy. I was dancing non-stop and singing."

"Why have you kept the red shoes?" she asked, though she already knew the answer.

"Part of me wants that happy time again…those red shoes are a reminder of that time."

"Why do you think you wore them on your trip here?"

Jennifer looked away, staring into a place only she could see.

Ingrid tried not to lose her. "Jennifer…Jennifer? Please come back and talk to me."

"Sorry…"

"Can you please tell me about the phone call?"

"Yes, the phone call… it was early morning. I knew it was Anita calling, with the three hours' time difference she's the only one that would call that early. Did I tell you Anita lives in New York?"

"Yes, you did."

Jennifer took a deep breath and began to recall that devastating phone call.

೮೦ ೮೦

"Anita, I'm so glad you called. I was thinking about you. How are things with you and Vincent?"

"Mom, I can't wait to show you my ring!" Anita said excitedly. "Do you like it?"

"I love it! And it's very, very pretty on my finger."

Jennifer couldn't help but smile. "I am so happy for you. By the way, I just bought the wine and champagne glasses for your engagement party."

"Mom, please make it simple –only close family and friends."

"I'll do my best. Are we still thinking July twelfth?" She had a wide grin on her face.

"Yes, Mom."

"We need to send the invitations out soon."

Anita changed the subject. "Mom, I think I found you the perfect boyfriend."

Jennifer bounced on her toes. "What are you talking about?"

"I am talking about Vincent's dad, Albert. Wouldn't it be funny if you two ended up together?"

"Where did you see his dad? I thought he lived in Paris."

"I'm joking! It would be crazy if my mom was with my fiancé's father." She was speaking in a bubbly tone.

Jennifer pressed her finger to her smiling lips. "Is Albert in New York?"

"Yes, he came for a visit."

Jennifer was curious. "How is Vincent's relationship with his dad?"

"I think he gets along with Jonathan better."

Jennifer took a deep breath and continued asking questions to get information. "How long have Jonathan and Rebecca been together?"

"Since Rebecca moved from Paris to New York with Vincent."

"How long ago was that?"

"Vincent was ten years old... you do the math."

"When did you meet Albert?" Her heartbeat increased.

"He's a famous artist. He was invited to have his art displayed in a prestigious art gallery in New York. There was a reception at the gallery for him. Vincent took me to the reception and introduced me to his dad."

Jennifer had an unrestrained smile. "Did you like him?"

"Very much. Mom, he is an *incredible* artist. You should see his work. The gallery was packed with so many people, and they were all in awe of his work. Didn't I tell you? He's a great boyfriend candidate!"

"Tell me everything about Albert. After all, he will be your father-in-law."

At this point in the call, Anita recounted her visit to the art gallery and meeting Albert. "Vincent, I can't believe your dad was invited to show his work in New York."

"He's a famous artist." He put his arm around Anita's shoulder and pulled her closer.

Anita raised her eyebrow. "Why didn't you tell me before?"

"I don't know. Maybe because of my mother," Vincent told her. "Why?"

Vincent opened his mouth to speak, paused to collect his thoughts, then continued. "Because she was hurt by my dad."

"How so?"

"Neither of them talk to me about it, so I figured it out myself. I could tell that my dad was in love with someone else."

Anita was persistent in her line of questions and curious to know more. "How did you find out?"

"When you see his paintings, you will see the yearning, the passion, the love."

"What are his paintings of?" Anita asked.

"The majority of his work is of a woman, the same woman."
He blew out a long breath.

"Maybe he was painting your mother."

"No, it's a different woman."

"How can you tell?"

"The color of the hair, the body type… the woman in the paintings is tall and slim." He tilted his head back, looking at the ceiling, letting out a heavy sigh.

Anita was intrigued. "I need to see them."

"We will go today around five p.m."

"Is the reception at that time?"

"Yes. The reception is from five to eight."

Anita became concerned about Vincent's feelings. She leaned forward, gave him a kiss, and continued. "How do you feel when you look at your father's paintings?"

"I don't know… Part of me is angry at him for not being emotionally available for my mom. Another part of me feels sorry for him."

"Do you think your mom would object to your dad being at our engagement party?"

Vincent rubbed his lips, thinking. "I don't know, maybe. She really loved my dad."

"Don't ever be like your dad and withdraw from me." Anita touched his hand.

"I would never do that. I know how much it hurt my mom." He pulled Anita closer.

"Your emotional connection with me is more important than our physical connection."

"Hey, you love my body, too." He gave her a deep belly laugh.

"You know what I mean…" Anita smiled at his teasing.

"I know, honey."

ജ ജ

Anita would graduate in May with an MBA degree, following in her mother's footsteps into the business world. She already had a job offer at a high-profile firm in New York. She was engaged to Vincent, who was in medical school. When Jennifer met Vincent two years ago, she knew he was the one for Anita.

Jennifer couldn't marry the man she loved, but her daughter would be marrying the man she loved and adored. Seeing Anita with Vincent, and the way they loved each other, was a kind of happy ending for Jennifer. At least she was able to provide for her daughter, pay for her education, and help her marry the man she loved.

And he was going to be a doctor. Her love, Babak, had planned to be a doctor.

From the time Jennifer met Vincent, it was like she was having her own engagement and wedding. But a different engagement party, one with a happy ending. She went to bridal shops looking at the gowns, imagining her daughter walking down the aisle with David by her side. She had already chosen the hotel she wanted for the wedding and reception.

The past two months, she had become more occupied with the engagement party. Anita wanted it to be held at Jennifer's home.

Babak had been in Jennifer's mind more than usual, as she relived the happy times she had shared with him.

ജ ജ

"Babak, please put me down. I am too heavy for you to carry me."

"Jennifer, I want to carry you on my shoulders for the rest of my life."

"I am embarrassed; please put me down. People are watching us."

"Honey, they are in envy of our love for each other."

"Jennifer!" Ingrid's sharp call interrupted Jennifer's deep thoughts. "You were talking to Anita. What did she tell you that made you leave town?"

Jennifer took in a deep breath, then expelled it to continue her story.

ଓ ଓ

"Anita, did you talk to his dad?"

"Yes, but at first I thought he was strange."

"Why is that?"

"He was very quiet, and just stared at me."

"Did you talk about this to Vincent?"

"Yes, he said it's because he is very private."

"Did he ask any questions?"

"Not during the reception."

"What did you do after the reception?"

"He took us to dinner."

"How was it?"

"It was like he kept wanting to say something, then he would stop himself and just stare at me."

"What did you think about his paintings?"

"I know Robert Watson's paintings speak to you. He often depicts just the back of one figure in his pieces, without showing the face. Albert's pieces all show a woman; you don't see her face, but she's tall with long black hair. Each painting shows her in a different position, whether it's jogging, walking, eating, drinking, cooking, holding a baby, pregnant… you name it. The paintings are all about her. It's very unique."

"Did he ask about your parents?"

"Yes, he asked when I was born."

"What else?"

"He asked for my mother's name."

"I am surprised he didn't know our names."

"Then he asked what you were doing."

"What else?"

"It was after dinner that he suddenly opened up."

"What did he say?"

"He said, 'I apologize for staring at you. You remind me of a girl I loved when I was going to university.'"

Jennifer said, "Poor Albert. Some of us have to suffer more than our share when it comes to love."

"Mom, at that moment, Vincent told his dad he wants to know about this love, the woman depicted in his paintings."

"What was his response?"

"He stayed quiet. Then Vincent said, 'The way you loved that woman. I want to know who she is and when you last saw her.'"

"Did he start talking about her?"

"Yes, Vincent and I stayed quiet. It was like the whole restaurant became quiet. He said, 'First of all, my sincerest apology to you, my son. I want you to know I tried to keep your mother and my marriage together, but my heart was aching for her. From the time we broke up, the ache never left me. Seeing both of you today brought back so much of my time with her. She had the most beautiful smile, long black hair… and her eyes. Those sparkling eyes. After so many years, I still hold her in my heart.'"

Vincent became impatient and interrupted his dad. "Dad, if you loved her so much, and you are still in love with her, why did you marry mom? It wasn't fair to her."

"It is not like that. I cared about your mom a lot."

"But you didn't love her." He rolled his eyes.

Albert took a long breath as he tried to find the right thing to say. "I think you are mature enough to know the whole story."

"Please, Dad… I want to know."

"Your mom and I were living in the same building. I was heartbroken, and your mom was grieving the loss of her fiancé due a tragic car accident. She was devastated. We would some-times get together and cry, sharing our heartbreak. Bit by bit we became closer, forming a good friendship. Then, as soon as you were born, we got married. Our marriage wasn't about love; it was more about parenthood and being there for each other as friends."

Albert continued, "After a while, your mom wanted more out of the relationship. I couldn't give that to her because my heart belonged to someone else. Someone who, even to this day, I believe loves me. I could feel her sadness, her joy, her grief. We had a kind of connection where there is no separation of time and space. All my paintings are about her emotion. When I feel it, I paint it."

"How about her with the baby?" He raised his eyebrow.

"The moment she gave birth, I knew. I painted her with the baby and many more throughout the years."

Vincent was asking pointed questions to better understand his dad. "If you two loved each other so much, why did you break up?"

"Family pressure. I was young and naïve and accepted the breakup in fear of hurting my parents." He let out a heavy sigh.

Anita was listening intensely to their conversation. She grabbed Vincent's hand under the table and softly caressed it.

Vincent continued. "Dad, what do you mean, family pressure?"

"They were against our relationship, and the family dynamic was different than what you experienced with your mom and me. We gave you the freedom to decide what you want in your life. I didn't have that freedom, and the guilt was enormous. I was afraid that if I moved ahead with our relationship, I would end up killing my mom, or at least, shortening her life."

"Dad, I don't understand." His voice rose.

Albert cleared his throat. "I know you don't, because I worked hard for you to not have this kind of guilt."

"What is this guilt about?"

"Feeling I was responsible for my mother's happiness."

Vincent softened his voice. "But…why?"

"It's cultural. In those days and in my family, a woman's self-worth was attached to the success of her children, their education, and marrying into a prominent family."

"But you married Mom. She wasn't from a distinguished family."

"I know. By the time I met your mom, I was heartbroken and depressed. I didn't care anymore. Your mom and I would get together for hours, both of us just crying and feeling sorry for ourselves."

"This is the part I don't understand. If you didn't care about your family anymore, why didn't you go after the woman you loved? Why didn't you convince her? Why did you give up? If Anita wanted to break up with me, I would do everything in my power for her to trust that she would have a happy life with me. What's missing here?"

Albert leaned forward and slid his chair closer, sighing heavily. "When I moved to Paris, I forgot to take my address book, and I didn't remember her home number to call her. I wrote letters to her almost every day. She never answered. Then, I got one of the letters back, postmarked return to sender, wrong address. I didn't know whether she had moved or if I had been writing to the wrong address all that time.

"After six months, I couldn't take it anymore and I went back to see her and to convince her to move with me to Paris. As soon as I arrived, I went to her home, but she no longer lived there. I contacted our friends, who said she was married and pregnant.

"I couldn't believe it. I wanted to see it for myself. I found out where she was living and spent two days across the street from her home waiting to see her. Finally, she came out of the house, prettier than ever, and pregnant. But so sad.

"I returned to Paris and have never been back, until this trip. And the only reason for me to come now was to see the two of you together, to make sure you truly love each other. The gallery show wasn't important to me. I have been invited many times in the past."

"Wow, Dad. You've gone through a lot. But forget about lost love, because we have the perfect match for you. Anita's mom Jennifer is great. She's attractive, highly educated, and single. You two would hit it off."

"So, the day has finally come when my son is setting me up. Ironically, the girl I loved, and still love, was named Jennifer, as well."

"Dad, I tell you…she will be the one that can make you forget about her…"

Anita jumped into the conversation. "Wait a minute. You're talking about my mother. This doesn't feel right for our parents to be together. We would be stepbrother and sister. It doesn't feel right."

"No worries, I was just kidding. Now that I am in love with you, I understand what my dad has gone through. I feel closer to him."

"I'm so sorry, Son, if I wasn't always there for you."

Jennifer became impatient at Anita's extended re-telling, and asked again, "Anita, did you ask Albert where he studied art?"

"In Paris. Mom, don't hang up. Vincent is about to leave and I need to ask him about the dinner at his parents' tonight."

Jennifer's gaze was bouncing from place to place. Her earlier smile vanished from her face, and she was very curious to know more about Albert. When Anita picked the phone back up, she asked, "Do you know where Albert met the girl he loved?"

"Do you mean Rebecca?"

Jennifer let out a heavy sigh. "No. I meant the girl in the paintings, the one that Albert was in love with."

"I think somewhere in France."

"What else do you know about Albert?"

"What's going on? Why are you so interested in Albert?"

"He is Vincent's father. I would like to get to know him better." Her fingers tapped the kitchen counter.

"Mom, you're starting to worry me now. He's a very nice man."

"Okay. That's good to know."

"Mom, I forgot to mention, I also met Albert's parents. They love Vincent very much. They also showed a lot of affection toward me. They asked about my parents, and when they found out how rich and successful you are, they seemed to like me more. Albert's mother was very curious and asked if I was Persian. She was very nosey and even asked if I knew any Persians. I told her, 'I'm sorry, my mom never associated with any Persians.'"

"Honey, your grandmother, Marguerite, is Persian." She shook her head.

"No, Mom, she was born there, but she's American, not Persian."

Jennifer opened her mouth to ask more questions, then stopped short. "Okay…what else?"

"They were very nice to me. Why don't you like Persians?" She spoke in a bubbly tone.

"What kind of question is that?"

"You never hired Persians at your companies."

"Most likely no Persians applied." She curled her toes.

"Mom, is it me, or are you discriminatory against Persians?"

"Stop it. It's not nice to talk like that."

"I don't know, it worries me that you have friends and employees from all over the world – except Persians."

Jennifer opened her mouth to speak, pausing to collect her thoughts, then she said "Don't worry."

"We have been on the phone for so long. I need to go soon."

"Okay, honey." She felt sad. She felt her body temperature rise, and the air was too thick to breathe.

"One more thing, Albert's mom loves Vincent very much. She praises him and they are so excited he's going to medical school. They are already calling him 'doctor'."

Anita continued, "She took me shopping yesterday. Mom, they are filthy rich. When we were shopping, she started talking about Albert and how much he hurt them because of a girl he met at the university. She said the girl was very poor and was after their money, pretending to be in love with Albert. Albert fell in love with her, and after they broke up, Albert moved to Paris.

Anita took a long breath, and with her smiling voice, continued. "She told me Albert was supposed to be a doctor, but that nasty, penniless girl made him crazy. He stopped going to medical school and stopped talking to them or seeing them until Rebecca and Albert were married. Rebecca helped make their relationship a little better.

"Mom, she was talking nonstop and blaming that girl so much for Albert moving to France."

Jennifer, in a panic, asked, "Anita, is Albert Persian?"

"Yes, Mom… Are you freaking out because Vincent's father is Persian?"

"Not at all. Where do Albert's parents live?" She held her hand over her heart.

"They have homes in several states, but they mostly live in California."

Jennifer asked the question that had a painfully obvious answer. "Do you know Albert's Persian name?"

"Of course I know. His signature is in Farsi. It's Babak."

Chapter 6

THE REBIRTH OF LOVE...

Ingrid's mouth was wide open after listening to Jennifer's retelling of her talk with her daughter. Jennifer had tears in her eyes. Ingrid covered her face with both hands, shaking her head. "I'm so sorry, Jennifer. I am so...so... sorry."

"I can't face it. I cannot break my daughter's heart. Anita and Vincent are brother and sister. Why does life have to be so cruel? Out of all the boys in the world, she has to fall in love with... her brother."

"But... you need to talk to them. At least you and Babak could have a happy ending. Anita is young. She'll find another love."

"The same way I found another love? I worked so hard to make sure money wouldn't keep her from marrying the man she loved, and now I have to do just that."

"I know it's hard, but you did everything in your power to let Babak know about your pregnancy."

"But I didn't tell Anita who her father is... Poor David."

"Yes, you'll have to talk to David. Perhaps the both of you can talk with... I don't know what I want to say."

The room became quiet. Neither of them said anything for a while. Ingrid finally got up and made chamomile tea, and they drank their tea in silence. Ingrid got up again. "I'm going to cook. Cooking calms my nerves."

Rob came into the house and ran to the kitchen with a beaming smile. "I need to share with you two ladies just how excited and happy I am."

Ingrid smiled. "Well…tell us all about it."

He took out his cell phone and handed it to Ingrid. "Check out these pictures."

"Where did you take these? What a beautiful garden. So many lush trees and flowers." She was scrolling through the pictures. "Wow! The waterfall picture is amazing. Where is this?"

"Close… Really, really close… It's Mr. and Mrs. Johnson's garden!"

"I can't believe it. It's one hundred times better than when the garden was in full bloom."

"I know. I'm very excited. I feel I initiated a good deed." Rob puffed his chest out a bit and grinned at his wife.

"How did you manage to do all that in such a short time?" Ingrid asked.

"Well, it was pretty great! First we cleared out the dead trees, dried plants, and flowers. Then we went to the nursery and picked up two trees and a few plants. None of us had a truck to move the trees, so I asked the owner if he could deliver them.

"When I gave him the address, he said, 'Do you mean Mr. and Mrs. Johnson's home?' I said yes and asked how he knew them. He said, 'Life is full of surprises. I bought this nursery from Mr. Johnson. He was very gracious to me when I started working here as a part-time employee. Soon after, I became a full-time employee. When Mr. Johnson decided to retire, he was very generous to strike a deal that I could afford to purchase the nursery.'

"Then, he showed me different plants and flowers, so many that I couldn't decide, and he called his landscaper over to help out. He told me he had learned everything from Mr. Johnson, who could bring life to almost any dead tree.

"When I asked what I owed him, he said 'zero', and that he'd been to Mr. and Mrs. Johnson's home and knew the garden. He even sent a few of his employees along with more plants, trees, and flowers."

Rob paused to take a breath, his cheeks pink with excitement. "I was amazed at all his generosity. And then he told me, 'This is my way of saying thank you for all the help Mr. Johnson gave me throughout the years.' And then he said he would pick out a fountain that best fit the Johnsons' yard and would deliver and set it up."

Ingrid laughed and took his hand. "Rob, I'm so proud of you." Then she gave him a kiss. "Please, come sit with us. I need to talk to you."

Rob took a seat, wondering what was going on, especially when he noticed how sad Jennifer appeared.

"Okay!" he blurted. "I know what's going on. We lost the house."

"No, no, no. It's not about the house," Ingrid said. Then she told Rob about Jennifer's phone call with her daughter, including that Anita and Vincent were brother and sister.

Rob listened; and his expression became sadder and sadder. He turned to Jennifer. "I am so sorry. I understand your terrible heartbreak now."

Jennifer had been silent throughout Ingrid's recounting and remained quiet now. Ingrid gently gripped Jennifer's wrist and to Rob, said, "Jennifer has to go back to talk to Babak. I don't want her to go alone. We need to be there for her. Rob, are you okay with us taking a trip to New York?"

"Of course, honey. But first, I think we need to ask Jennifer if she wants us to tag along."

Jennifer quickly looked up at Rob. "If you two were with me, it would make it so much easier. Otherwise, I'm afraid I won't have the courage to face it, knowing how much my daughter will be hurt."

Rob gave her a firm nod. "From here to New York is about seven hours' drive. I will be your driver."

"You're such a good driver," Ingrid said.

Rob got up and said, "I need a quick shower after all that garden work. Please, excuse me." He kissed Ingrid's forehead and went upstairs.

Soon after, the doorbell rang. Ingrid left the kitchen and opened the door to a stranger, who said, "Are Mr. or Mrs. Thompson home?"

Ingrid hesitated a moment. "I'm sorry. They don't live here."

"Do you know where they moved to?"

"Philadelphia...some time ago..."

"Do you have their address? I'm a friend of the family and it's very important that I reach them."

"Wait a minute. Let me see if I can find the address." Ingrid closed the door and came back to the kitchen.

"Jennifer, a man is at the door looking for your dad or your mom. He said he's a friend of the family. Should I give him your parents' address?"

"Let me go see who it is."

Curious about who might be looking for her parents, Jennifer went to the door and opened it. "Babak!"

"Jennifer?"

As soon as they saw each other, it was like nothing had changed. The world became still, and they leapt into each other's arms, embracing and kissing.

Ingrid became curious about the man at the door and concerned about Jennifer, so she headed for the front door. She made it to the doorway to the living room, where she saw the half-open front door and Jennifer and the stranger in an intense embrace.

"This man must be Babak. Finally, Jennifer will face the truth."

Ingrid returned to the kitchen and started preparing dinner. A half hour or so later, Rob walked down the stairs. Jennifer pulled away from Babak's arms and said, "Babak, let me introduce you to my good friend, Rob."

After the introduction, they walked towards the kitchen. Ingrid was busy cooking, but as soon as she saw them, she went to Babak, shook his hand, and said, "I'm Ingrid. You must be Babak."

Before Babak could say anything, Jennifer said, "Ingrid and Rob have been such a great help to me during this difficult period of my life."

Babak nodded, barely able to take his eyes from Jennifer long enough to acknowledge Ingrid, who waved them all toward the table to sit. Then she said, "Let's have a glass of wine to celebrate Babak and Jennifer's reunion."

"I'll drink to that," Babak immediately replied. "I've waited so long for this moment."

Jennifer had tears in her eyes and her two friends were concerned about her bringing up the news of Anita and Vincent being brother and sister. Jennifer stayed silent though, so Ingrid started things off. "Babak, why did you want to talk to Mr. and Mrs. Thompson?"

"I wanted to find Jennifer. I thought she might be hiding at her parents' home."

"Did you ask Vincent or Anita where she was?" Ingrid asked.

"Yes. All of us were trying to figure out where she was. She wasn't at work or her home. Anita said she talked to her grandparents, and they said she wasn't with them. Anita didn't mention her grandparents moving to Philadelphia. I thought they still lived in Erie."

Jennifer interjected, "I never brought Anita to Erie, only Philadelphia."

Babak said, "Now I remember. I asked her if they were in the same house and she said 'yes.'"

"Babak, do they know about us?"

"Of course, my love. I couldn't hide my excitement from them."

"How was their reaction?"

"They were happy for us."

Jennifer froze for a moment, then whispered, "Anita is…" But didn't finish.

Ingrid noticed this, but Babak, sitting next to her, didn't.

Ingrid tapped the table with her fingers and said, "Babak, tell us about your trip to New York, and how you met Anita."

Babak glanced at Ingrid, smiled, and said, "Well, it began in this way… When I met Anita at the gallery reception, my heart dropped. She looked so much like Jennifer. Same dark hair and brown eyes. I couldn't believe the similarities to the girl I have loved for so many years. I wanted to find out if she was Jennifer's daughter. I think I made her uncomfortable because I kept staring at her.

"Later that night, I took Anita and Vincent to dinner. I was curious and had so many questions. I started with asking her when she was born, which convinced me even more that she might be Jennifer's daughter…especially when I found out that Anita's mother's name was Jennifer.

"I continued with my questions, like what her mother does, and Anita said her mother was a businesswoman who had her own company. That gave me some doubt, so I asked if her mother's hobby was painting. The answer was disappointing, as she said her mother never painted and had no interest in painting. That she was all about business and making money.

"I told myself my Jennifer never would quit painting. My Jennifer wasn't all about money. And with that, I gave up the wishful thinking of Anita's mom being my Jennifer and having my own happy ending.

"At the gallery reception, David had been introduced to me as Anita's father. He was very engaged with my paintings. He showed such a great interest. Then he said, 'Your signature is Babak, a Persian name. Are you Persian?'

"'Yes. I am. Babak was my name before I moved to Paris.'

"'Did you go to UC Berkeley?'

"'Yes.'

"'Were you in love with a girl named Jennifer?'

"'Yes.'

"As soon as I said that, he became pale. I thought something was wrong with him. Then, he immediately excused himself and hurried out of the gallery, while saying, 'Oh my. Oh my.'

"Anita ran after him, asking, 'Dad, what happened? Are you leaving?'

"He told her he thought he might have gotten a bug and was going home to rest.

"Three days later he called me, saying he needed to talk to me and offered to meet for a coffee.

"I assumed he was a concerned father and wanted to get to know me better. He chose a very quiet place, and after we shook hands, he dropped into one of the chairs. It was obvious he wasn't feeling well. His eyes were puffy, and he looked very worried. I asked him what was going on and if everything was okay with the two lovebirds.

"'Yes, they're fine.'

"'Then, what's going on?'

"'I'm sick to my stomach.'

"'Oh…?'

"'Since the reception, I can't sleep. I can't eat. I love my girl. I love her so much, and I know I have to break her heart.'

"'What are you talking about?'

"'I wish her mother was available to talk to me. But I think she found out the truth, couldn't deal with it, and ran away. No one knows where she is. I'm worried about her, too.'

"'What truth?'

"'Anita's mother is the same Jennifer you loved.'

"My heart dropped, and I had a big smile. I told him I had been wishing for such great news and not to worry, that I would find Jennifer.

"But he was still upset, saying, 'No. It's not great news. I love my daughter. I can't break her heart. I was there when she was born. Her first words, her first steps, when her baby teeth fell out. She is my life. I can't break her heart.'

"'I don't understand. Did Vincent tell you he's breaking up with Anita?' He raised an eyebrow.

"David looked exhausted and strained to the limit. 'I wish I could find Jennifer. I know how much she loves Anita. Jennifer is in pain and is hiding. I hope she doesn't hurt herself.'

"At that point, I became impatient and said, 'Whatever it is, tell me. Why is Jennifer in pain?'

"'I want to tell you. But I'm Anita's father. I don't want to lose her.' He was staring down at his feet.

"I leaned forward. 'I will be her father-in-law. You won't lose her.'

"'We need to stop their marriage.' He laid a hand against his heart and sighed.

"'They love each other. Why stop their marriage?'

"'Because... they are brother and sister.' His eyes welled up.

"'What?'

"'Anita is your daughter.'

"He started crying and I took his hand in mine to say, 'The wedding will go on.'

"'We cannot.'

Babak's eyes were soft and filled with an inner glow.

"'Yes, we can.'

"'How?'

"'Vincent is not my biological son.' He had a wide grin on his face.

"Then, to reassure David that he would still be Anita's father, I told him that I understood the feelings he had for Anita, because I had the same feelings for Vincent, and our love for them would never change."

Rob pulled Ingrid up off her chair, snapped on the small radio sitting on the kitchen counter that was eternally tuned to an easy listening music station, and with a big grin said, "With news like this, we need to dance. Let's dance."

They all began dancing around the kitchen. When the song ended, Jennifer pulled Babak's hand and said, "Let's sit. I have so many questions."

"Okay, my love."

"Did you tell Vincent and Anita the truth?"

"No. I spoke with Rebecca and we decided we would wait until you were back. Rebecca, Jonathan, and I will break the news to Vincent. You, David, and I will let Anita know. David has been such a great father to Anita, and he truly loves her."

"He's an amazing, kind-hearted man," Jennifer said.

"He told me everything about your fake marriage, and the way you were treated by my mother when you went to give her the news of your pregnancy."

"Yes, it was very harsh, my love." Jennifer looked at his hands in hers and smiled. "We need to go to New York. David needs to know nothing will change for him. But I'm worried about how the kids will react. If Anita will become angry and upset with me and David for not telling the truth about her father."

"They will be okay, don't worry."

Jennifer was still confused about something. "Do you know how David figured out that you were the same Babak? He never saw you."

"With tears in his eyes, he told me that as soon as he saw my dimples he knew, because his beautiful girl had the same dimples."

"Babak, tell me about Rebecca. How did you two meet?"

Babak took a deep breath. "Rebecca was my neighbor in France. She was living with her fiancé, Victor, two doors down from my apartment. When I moved in with my uncle Bijan and my cousin Ardashir, Rebecca and Victor came to our door and introduced themselves and welcomed us to the building. Both were students at the same university I was enrolled in. Victor was also the super for the building, so we would call him for any type of maintenance.

"After six months in Paris, I decided to go back to Berkeley for a visit. I was determined to find you, my love, and bring you back with me to Paris. During our six-month stay in Paris, Ardashir wasn't happy. Learning the language was too difficult for him and he begged his father to go back to Canada. The same day I left for Berkeley, they left for Canada.

"The day I saw you pregnant was the worst day of my life. I flew back to Paris and never came back until this recent trip to New York. When I arrived back in Paris, I stayed in my room for a couple of days. When I decided to take a shower, there wasn't hot water, so I knocked on Rebecca and Victor's apartment door.

"Rebecca opened the door and was in bad shape. I asked for Victor, saying I had no hot water, but before I could finish, she told me Victor had died in a car accident.

"I sat down in the door, holding my legs, and started bawling. I knew Rebecca was heartbroken. It was always so obvious how much they loved each other. With our combined heartbreaks and loss, it seems I lost control of myself. Rebecca was surprised and asked if I was okay, but I couldn't move or speak or stop crying. Finally, Rebecca told me to come inside.

"I inched into her apartment, still sobbing. She gave me a glass of water, told me to take a few deep breaths. For a while both of us were quiet. Then I shared with Rebecca my heartbreak about you, seeing you pregnant with another man's child. Rebecca shared the pain and agony of losing Victor, and how much they loved each other. Then she told me she was pregnant.

"From that day on we became good friends, sharing our sorrows, and sometimes having a good cry together.

"One day she came to my place and said, 'I want to share with you that I have decided to place my baby up for adoption. I talked to some agencies and one of them has a very good family that they thought would be a good match.' I was surprised that she could give up her child. She went on to tell me, 'This child is Victor's baby. I loved Victor so much that I want his child to have

209

the love and comfort of a mother and father, not just me. I am not working. I have no means of supporting myself and my child, and my family is not financially able to support us.'

"That day I did everything to change her mind. But she was determined to put her baby up for adoption. I wasn't going to school anymore, so I painted all day and night. And, of course, my subject was you. My parents still thought I was in medical school and lavished me with money.

"Rebecca and I still got together for an occasional meal or tea. More days passed by. She was the cook and I would wash the dishes. Her belly was getting bigger and bigger. One night, she started crying and blurted out, 'I cannot do it. I cannot give up my baby.' I held her hand and said, 'How about I become the father of your baby?' My question was such a relief for her. She hugged me and said, 'Thank you. Thank you.'

"I was there when Vincent was born, and the moment I looked at him, I loved him. I think I have been a good father to Vincent, and I love him dearly as my son, even though he is not my biological son. So, I do understand what David is going through.

"Rebecca, bit by bit, became jealous of my paintings and wanted me more emotionally connected to her, but I could not give up the love I had for you. Finally, Rebecca gave up. She fell in love with Jonathan. It seems they have a happy life."

Babak got up from his chair and said, "I need to take care of something before the stores close. I will be back soon." He turned to Ingrid. "Where is the nearest department store?"

Ingrid gave him directions and Jennifer followed him to the door. Babak took her in his arms and whispered in her ear, "I will call Anita and Vincent; you call Elizabeth to let her know you are okay. She was very worried about you."

After he left, Ingrid called for her to come back to the kitchen, and as she walked in, Rob said, "I'm hungry. Let's eat."

Jennifer smiled at him, then looked at Ingrid, who wore a Cheshire cat smile. "What's going on?"

Ingrid clasped her hands together. "Babak went to buy you an engagement ring."

"Did he tell you that?" Jennifer's tone was one of disbelief.

Ingrid shook her head and laughed. "No. I just know. What else could be so urgent that he would leave his reunited love to go to a department store?"

Jennifer smiled shyly. "I hope so..."

Rob hovered near the stove. "He won't be back for at least an hour. I'm hungry. We can eat now and leave food for Babak or I can eat and you two can wait for him."

"You go ahead, honey. I know you worked up an appetite with all you did today. We'll wait. Jennifer and I are going to chat a bit."

That said, she pulled Jennifer to a chair and gestured for her to sit. "Jennifer, I think even if he doesn't come back with a ring tonight, you need to propose to him."

"Do you think so?"

"Yes, I do. I'm sure of it. You two have waited so long. I think you need to get married here, before going to New York and breaking the news to the kids."

"I can't get married without Anita."

"Yes, you can. You don't need to delay your own happiness for even a minute more."

"I don't know."

"Girl, listen to me. Ask him to marry you. We will have the ceremony in Mr. and Mrs. Johnson's garden. I will be your maid of honor and Rob will be the best man. The nine families you helped will do everything necessary for you two to have an unforgettable wedding. It might not be luxurious but it will be filled with love."

Jennifer hesitated. "I'd like to have a wedding here, but if he doesn't ask me, I'm not comfortable asking him."

"Listen to me, you need to get married before leaving for New York. Twenty-five years of separation is enough for both of you." Ingrid stabbed the tabletop with her finger for emphasis.

"Okay. Okay. If he doesn't ask me, I'll ask him… under one condition…"

"What's that?"

"You and Rob come with us to New York."

"Are you sure?"

"Of course I'm sure."

Babak rang the doorbell. Jennifer ran to him and opened the door with a big smile. They hugged and exchanged a big kiss. With Babak's arms around her, they entered the kitchen.

Before Ingrid or Rob could say a word, Babak took Jennifer's hand and went to one knee before her.

"Jennifer Thompson. Love of my life. Would you marry me and make me the happiest man in the whole world?"

Jennifer opened her mouth, then smiled enormously and said, "Wait a minute…"

She hurried to the front door, where she had left her red shoes. Snatching them up, she slipped them on and nearly ran back to the kitchen.

"Babak. Ask me again."

The End

Made in the USA
Las Vegas, NV
23 February 2021